What People Are Saying About

Amanita Virosa

Amanita Virosa is a triumph of storytelling, a testament to the enduring spirit of the oppressed and their determination to stand up for what is right, no matter the cost. Based on actual political events in 90s London, this novel deserves a place on every bookshelf and in the hearts of those who believe in the power of the people to effect change.

Carlton Duncan, British educator and author of *True Determination*

What truly sets *Amanita Virosa* apart is its ability to inspire. Harden's book serves as a powerful reminder that the fight for justice is never futile, no matter how insurmountable the odds may seem. This is not just an edge-of-your-seat, thrill ride but an elucidating, affecting commentary on ordinary citizens' struggles to regain their dignity against overwhelming odds. Barry Harden is a master storyteller with the rare ability to entertain, educate, and inspire simultaneously.

Daniel Ramos, author of *Fighting for Honor* and Historynet contributor

Amanita Virosa

The Destroying Angel

Amanita Virosa

The Destroying Angel

Barry Harden

ROUNDFIRE
BOOKS

London, UK
Washington, DC, USA

CollectiveInk

First published by Roundfire Books, 2025
Roundfire Books is an imprint of Collective Ink Ltd.,
Unit 11, Shepperton House, 89 Shepperton Road, London, N1 3DF
office@collectiveinkbooks.com
www.collectiveinkbooks.com
www.roundfire-books.com

For distributor details and how to order please visit the 'Ordering' section on our website.

Text copyright: Barry Harden 2023

ISBN: 978 1 80341 681 6
978 1 80341 694 6 (ebook)
Library of Congress Control Number: 2023947160

A CIP catalogue record for this book is available from the British Library.

Design: Lapiz Digital Services

UK: Printed and bound by CPI Group (UK) Ltd, Croydon, CR0 4YY
Printed in North America by CPI GPS partners

We operate a distinctive and ethical publishing philosophy in all areas of our business, from our global network of authors to production and worldwide distribution.

Foreword

In the heart of North London, amidst the grey urban sprawl and bustling streets, lies a story that reverberates with the echoes of defiance, resistance, and revolution. These pages recount a tale of ordinary people challenged by extraordinary circumstances in a story that is loosely based on actual political events which unfolded in the early nineties.

Barry Harden's narrative invites you to step into Everard's world, an indigent young man whose ire smouldered within him, stoked by mistreatment at the hands of the police and fuelled by the blatant extortion of citizens by uncontrolled mobsters. At the tale's centre stands a remarkable Roma woman hailing from the turbulent lands of Bosnia-Herzegovina. Unwittingly, she becomes a participant in a mini revolution that would shake the very foundations of her adopted country.

Amanita's journey begins in the midst of the Balkan Wars at a time of unfathomable violence, displacement, and despair. Amidst the chaos of a homeland torn apart by conflict, Amanita sows the seeds of anarchy, her spirit unyielding even in the face of unimaginable horrors. Her courage is born from necessity, and her defiance, a response to the oppressive forces that seek to extinguish her identity and freedom.

Amanita finds herself transplanted to North London, a place far removed from the blood-soaked soil of her youth, yet one that carries its own set of challenges and injustices. In a city divided by class, race, and socioeconomic disparities, she discovers a community united by shared struggles. The fire of resistance that once burned within her is rekindled as she witnesses the injustices faced by those around her. And in this multicultural, vibrant enclave of North London, the stage is set for a revolution of small yet profound proportions.

Through the pages of this novel, you will be transported to the streets of London, to the hideaways where plans are hatched, to the passionate voices raised in protest, and to the hearts of individuals who refuse to accept the status quo. You will bear witness to a powerful alliance of people from all walks of life, drawn together by the magnetic force of Amanita's and Everard's indomitable spirits and their unwavering commitment to justice.

As you immerse yourself in the unfolding narrative, you will come to understand that revolutions are not always grand, and heroes are not always invincible. Sometimes they are ordinary individuals who rise to the occasion when their circumstances demand it. They are people who refuse to remain silent, who dare to challenge the powers that be and who, against all odds, ignite a spark of change that cannot be extinguished, even when their individual voices are snuffed out.

In the pages that follow, you will embark on a journey of resilience, sacrifice, and hope, of violence and defiance, love and loss, and the enduring power of the human spirit in a world where the ordinary becomes extraordinary.

In the realm of literature, there are writers, and then there are those rare luminaries who not only craft brilliant narratives but also wield their words as weapons against the darkness of social injustice and government indifference. It is with great enthusiasm and anticipation that I introduce you to the work of an author who embodies this rare breed, a writer unafraid to speak his mind, to illuminate the shadows, and to expose the rot of corruption that sometimes festers within the very heart of the state.

Harden's pen is mightier than any sword, for it cuts through the layers of obfuscation and deceit that can shroud the corridors of power. In the pages of his works, you will find incisive commentary on sociopolitical veritas artfully concealed beneath the veneer of riveting, action-laden narratives. His words are not swayed by political expediency or personal gain; they are fuelled by a burning desire for justice, equality, and tolerance. But beyond the critique lies a profound sense of empathy and a vision of a more just society, one where every voice is heard and every living thing is valued.

As you delve into the pages of *Amanita Virosa*, you will be challenged to confront uncomfortable truths, to question the decisions of those in power, and to reflect on the role each of us plays in the collective struggle for a fairer, more compassionate world. His narratives are not merely stories; they are mirrors held up to our society, reflecting both its beauty and its flaws.

Harden's writing is a testament to the enduring power of literature to shine a light on the darkest corners of society and to ignite the flames of change.

As you embark on this literary journey, prepare to be moved, to be challenged, and to be inspired. Welcome to the world of a brilliant writer whose words become a force for change, and where the pursuit of justice is a noble and unwavering quest.

Isabel López
Author, *Isabel's Hand-Me-Down Dreams*
New York, NY
September 15, 2023

Chapter 1

It's only when everything, absolutely everything has gone wrong that one has to make a positive decision. Everard, sitting in the shade of an ancient chestnut tree, had reached that point. In front of him, he had laid out all of his possessions: a penknife, a length of rope, a toy pistol and its plastic silencer, an old cheese sandwich and, of course, his dog, his precious Molly.

Was any money there? No. Not a sou.

Was there any hope? No. Not one jot.

He looked at the tree, then at the rope. *That would be easy*, he thought. Then he looked at Molly. *Who would take care of her? Nobody. She would starve. Could they share the same noose? No. It was not her fault. So who's fault was it? His!*

Of course it was his—Dorkin, the money lender! He was the cause of all the trouble, and Everard was not going to let him take it out on Molly. Everard had acted as guarantor for a close friend on a loan of £3,000 from Dorkin. Unfortunately, the untimely death of that friend in a road accident had left Everard not only accountable for the original sum but also the other £6,400 in interest. Everard lost everything he possessed, and under the circumstances, his partner decided to bid him farewell too. The only thing that Everard was left with was Molly and that was only because she was not really saleable, or so it was decided by the bailiffs.

It is sometimes difficult to comprehend that in some cases starvation and deprivation can have a positive effect on the mental functioning of some adults. Hunger can sharpen the wits and desperation can throw caution aside. As a result, focus is sometimes elevated, and the physical ability of that unfortunate can be enhanced. A thin man can usually run faster than a fat one for example, and Everard was now definitely not fat. He had lost all his excess with the exception of his hair, which had grown from a crop to a cluster of dark, curly locks around his neck, slightly matted and not a little greasy. But that is what happens, and there he was ... still alive!

Everard opened the knife and cut the sandwich in two. He held out half to Molly who ate it with one quick snap. Everard looked at the other piece and decided he was not hungry. Molly lingered for a moment, cocking her head to one side.

"Everard," she asked, "Why don't you want it? What's the matter?"

"You have it, Molly. I've got to work something out and it's best I do it on an empty stomach."

"But you didn't eat anything yesterday either."

"I know, but I was really down and didn't know what to do."

"Okay. I give in. You better hand it over before it dries up."

Molly carefully removed the remaining portion from Everard's hand and swallowed it very slowly as if she didn't really want to take it. They sat there for some time, Molly with her chin on her paws and Everard deep in thought. The clouds, which had enveloped the morning with a gloom that seemed to match Everard's mood, had slightly thinned. A trace of sunlight could be seen traveling across the field and alighting on the fallen leaves which had just begun to moulder on the ground around the two of them.

Everard looked up from his reverie, gazed directly into Molly's eyes and slowly whispered, "Now Molly, stand up ... sit down ... stand up ... fall over. Now, if I point the gun at you and it goes bang, I want you to fall over as if you were dead. Right, are you ready? Shall we try it again? We need to get this absolutely right!"

Molly didn't look like the brightest of mongrels. She was slightly overweight from a poor diet of whatever scraps she could find, mainly from outside the many junk food outlets that then festooned the high street. Nonetheless she was ready.

She was always a quick learner and soon, the two of them had worked out Everard's revenge.

***

It's one thing to have a plan, but it's another thing to get it right. Planning the plan is essential. Monday morning, outside the post office at 8.45 a.m., the first limousine pulled up. Dorkin the extortioner waited for his door to be opened by his chauffeur, trundled his grossness onto the pavement, and spat his half-smoked cigar into the gutter. He smirked to himself as the victims of his trade dragged their misery to queue outside the post office, again in the rain, dreading the cold hand of the money lender fishing in their bags to steal their meagre allowance, leaving them again in his praying-mantis clutches.

One such victim was Mrs. Wells, a woman in her mid-sixties. Everard, who had arrived with Molly soon after 8 a.m., noticed her in particular. He noticed the anger in her scowl when she spotted Dorkin arrive. It was obvious that she had spirit and loathed the man who grew so obese on the blood of her fellows in the queue.

Doris Wells had hoped to be in and out of the post office, her pension secured in her handbag before Dorkin arrived. But he knew it, and he also knew that the shop wouldn't be open until five past nine. That's what the £20 a week to Gilbert the cashier in the post office was for—making them wait.

The trickle of pensioners grew, all forsaken by the rises in the cost of living, dragging their misery along to join the others, each one indebted to one or the other of the fat men and women whose big cars lined the broad pavement regardless of any parking restrictions. They owned not only the pensioners but had in their thrall most of the wardens and community police officers who pretended to guard the interests of the people and the law.

Everard sat with Molly and watched from a doorway a little way down the street. He noted the car numbers and looked out for the debris cast carelessly out of the car windows, which might give some clue as to the destinations or places of entertainment that the sharks might visit.

The post office opened at last, and the old folks tottered in, stiff with the wait in the cold of a winter morning. They lingered awhile before leaving, wrapping scarves around their faces. Some even swapped coats in an attempt to avert the robbery that they surely would suffer once they were outside again.

"Morning, Mrs. Wells. Glad to see you're up so early, just like me. Early bird, you know. So let me see. Ah, what a shame! It was due at 9 a.m. sharp, and here we are at quarter past. I'm afraid you have therefore incurred a penalty. It means, as you can see in our contract, that should any payments be made later than the specified time, then you have added to your debt an extra week's repayment due at the end of this week. If you have any trouble finding the money, I suggest you go to Mr. Wragge over there and raise the necessary funds from him. I'm sure he will accommodate you."

As they left, few of the pensioners escaped the clutches of the sharks. Even those who had no debts were cross-examined as to how they could survive without being owned by the parasites that had swallowed their lives and property.

Everard noted every one whose purse was emptied. But he focused on Mrs. Wells, and during the following days, he watched to see where she lived and how dire her circumstances had become. Nobody would question him. After all, who exactly was he? Just another homeless twenty-four-year-old whose life was turned upside down. Like so many others, he slept on the streets, ate from soup kitchens, and was deserted by the state and public alike.

He was often moved on by the police, frequently pushed around and jeered at. "Scum rat, benefit cheat, lazy pisshead."

Yes, and they had done that too, urinated on him as he slept and always went away laughing. Benefits? He had none. He wasn't entitled. Dorkin had claimed that there was still money owing but ceased to recognise Everard since his decline into destitution and seemed less interested in hounding him.

"There's no more blood left in that stone," Everard heard him say to Wragge one day. "That's the trouble with that sort. All losers putting friendship above money, total rubbish! But he still owes me, and I won't forget it, just in case he gets on his feet again. I'll soon put an end to that with all the interest he'll have to find. What a waste of space! I'd charge him for the air he breathes if I could."

Everard had traced Mrs. Wells's address and most of the others', following them distantly as they dragged their dissolution home each Monday morning, ever colder and hungrier, reduced to starvation by the minions of the big society.

Dorkin and Wragge were part of the big society. Their friends, the Randolphs, the Spurns, and the Honeylickers were the big society, and they all lived off the despair of those sucked under by the great state confusion. But it didn't stop there. There was nothing to stop it, except Everard and Molly.

Suddenly, the chance was there—the shiny black Lexus, its paintwork gleaming in the dim streetlight just a few paces down the road from Twenty-to-One, the bookies on Lennox Street. As they watched, the lights of the shop were extinguished, and they could see Dorkin pulling down the shutter to the window.

"Molly, now's the time. Up the road with you, keep hidden, and wait for the sign."

Molly went quickly into the shadows, past the door, and sat quietly behind a car until the call came.

Dorkin took his time. He had drunk quite a lot while he was gathering his takings along with the contents of the safe and staggered towards his motor clutching a leather satchel close to his chest. It had been a bumper day for him, having sucked the last pennies from almost all of the punters that passed their days in the Twenty-to-One.

Everard stepped out to block his way just as Molly sidled up alongside the fat leech. "Hand it over or I'll shoot your dog!" Everard shouted.

Dorkin looked down and sneered, "I haven't got a dog, scumbag!"

Everard pointed the gun at Molly and pulled the trigger. There was a muffled bang as the slightly damp cap exploded with a small puff of smoke. But it was enough. Molly keeled over, making a single squeak as she went. Dorkin was horrified and dropped the satchel.

"Pick it up, or I'll kill you too. Do it!" Everard jabbed Dorkin in the ribs with the silencer of the toy pistol. Dorkin bent forward, but his greed-fed obesity dragged him down and he fell face first onto the waiting paving stones.

"Help me! Help me! Please help me!" he gasped, rolling over onto his back and clutching his left arm. "My pills ... pills ... in the satchel ... quick, quick!"

Everard pulled the satchel away from Dorkin's reach. He lowered the gun to the head of the struggling gargoyle.

"Don't you remember me? Everard ... Everard Tilson? You destroyed me. You took everything from me, absolutely everything, and now you're going to pay."

Everard pulled the trigger again, and in that instant, Dorkin lost his terror and died of fright. Molly jumped up from the ground, and the two slipped nimbly away into the darkness of the night.

***

Wednesday morning was cold, dark, and wet. Dripping, Everard stood with Molly outside the door of Mrs. Wells's council flat and rang the bell.

"Who is it?" came the frail voice.

"I am looking for Mrs. Wells. I have a package for her."

She opened the door with the chain still fixed in position, allowing a smitch of the coldness from within to enter the dank corridor that led to the stairs.

"I don't know you. Go away! I'll call out if you don't."

"Mrs. Wells. I am a friend and have something for you that you really do need. I have some money for you. Come, let me in and turn the fire up. You'll be able to keep yourself warm from now on."

Dorkin's satchel had been well stuffed, fifties and twenties, tens and fives. They were in bundles of one hundred notes, and altogether, there were around forty or so bundles. Everard couldn't be bothered to count it. He wasn't that interested in the amount, but he knew it was a small fortune. He gave Mrs. Wells enough to keep her out of mischief for the rest of her life. Five rolls of fifties and ten of twenties, enough not to be squandered but enough to feed, clothe and keep herself warm. It was enough to lift her spirits and for her to breathe more easily.

"Would you like a cup of tea?" she stuttered as she gazed in amazement at the pile of notes.

"That would be nice … and some for Molly, please."

"Does she have it in a cup or a bowl?"

"In a cup, please."

***

Everard was not finished but needed a base from which to work. He bought some clothes from charity shops and had his hair cut and his beard shaved. He found a small basement flat on the cheap side of town and set up a stall at the local market selling supermarket goods at half the price to pensioners only. It caused a minor stir with some but was generally accepted by the other stall holders. Nobody questioned him. They assumed that he was charity funded. Nobody knew the truth, not even Mrs. Wells.

What about Wragge? Yes! What about him? He was still there, doing what he did. He was not so careless nor as fat as Dorkin, but he was just as greedy.

Wragge didn't do it himself, but he gave Mrs. Dorkin a serious fright when she found the corpse of her late husband, once so carefully laid out, lying face down on the carpet in the undertaker's funerary room. His coffin was more or less destroyed, the linings and paddings shredded with screws and splinters left lying all over the floor.

Of course, it was the book that Wragge wanted — the list of names that owed Dorkin money. But it wasn't there. In fact, it was nowhere, just like the money, vanished.

Mrs. Dorkin received another call, this time at her home. It was Wragge, who brought her flowers and a cheap box of chocolates hoping that she would fall for his charms. But she didn't because not only did he lack any charm, but she had no idea as to what he was asking.

Flustered, Wragge responded, "What do yer mean, you don't know what he was up to? You've been living off it for long enough. Just look at this place. It's like a bloody palace! Look here, it's a notebook, a little black one with some names in it, that's all. That's all I want. He said I could have it one day. So I'm here and I want it!"

She looked at him quizzically. "The only book I ever saw him with was his diary. But you don't want to look in there. I've read some of it. He wrote in it a couple of weeks ago just before he died, something like, 'Wragge is a greedy bastard, and I think I need to watch him.' So what do you think of that? Are you a greedy bastard, Mr. Wragge? Are you the one that caused him to die? Are you? It's strange that he wrote that and now he's dead, don't you think?"

Wragge rose, gathered up the chocolates and flowers, and marched out. On his way back to his office, he called in at the florist and demanded his money back and not without threats.

Everard had seen the book. He had even used it but only to track and repay all those who had suffered under Dorkin's levy. He followed Wragge for several weeks but could find no means of catching him off-guard. Molly had played her part brilliantly, but this time, there was no chance for a second performance. Well, not with this one, that was for sure.

He had lost contact with Mrs. Wells for some weeks and thought maybe that the time was right to pay her another visit to see how she was getting on. She was delighted to see him and called him in for a cup of tea and a piece of cake.

What surprised him was that she was not as short as he had always visualised her, not five feet three but definitely taller and even a little stockier at a substantial five feet seven. He pondered for a second or two, *Has she grown or is it my imagination?*

"I'm moving," she said. "Not far, though. Just up to Tottenham. Second floor flat. I'll be glad not to have to go up so many stairs again. Eight stories, it's just too much for my old pins. And it's all thanks to you. I don't know how I can ever repay you."

"You make me sound like Mr. Dorkin or even Mr. Wragge with a phrase like that." Everard laughed.

"Oh, that Mr. Wragge. He's an evil piece of work! Makes Dorkin look like a saint. I'd love to see him come a cropper. You know he has had some of his debtors beaten up and actually robbed them in the street. The police don't do a thing. Sometimes they hold the victim while Dorkin goes through their pockets. And if you're a female, he has his hand up your front, pulls your bra about. I've even seen him go up a young woman's skirt pretending to be looking for money. Then he always goes off laughing."

Everard thought for a moment. "Given the chance, Mrs. Wells, say you were a bit younger, would you try to get rid of him?"

"Kill him, do you mean? Well, he does deserve it, all the misery he's caused. Yes, I suppose I would. It's worth thinking about, isn't it. Why? Have you got something in mind?"

"How many tenants in this block owe him money?"

"Nearly all of them. I think I'm the only one who's caught up with him. Why?"

"What if you take on a debt with him and get him to call round to collect. You know, skip a repayment. That'll get him hot. From what you say, he hates people who miss their repayments. But what's important is that you give him an address on one of the top floor flats on this side of the block. Mind you, if what I have in mind goes wrong, I think he could be really nasty."

"And?"

"Well, when he arrives to give you some grief, you will be down here and out of his sight. When he reaches your supposed door, you will need to call out from below, 'Mr. Wragge, Mr. Wragge, I'm so sorry. I can't get up the stairs too quickly.' He'll then lean over the balcony to shout abuse at you and tell you how much extra you are going to have to pay. I will slip out of the door of the flat behind him, grab his ankles, and tip him over the rail.

"Be ready to get out of the way because he'll be coming down quite fast. But remember, timing is absolutely essential. Make sure he's at the upstairs door before you call out. Also, and this is really important, make a friend of someone on that top landing if you haven't already got one, and invite them down to tea at the appointed time. I'll need that floor to be empty so I can get him over the balcony without being seen."

"D'you think it'll work?"

"We'll only know if we give it a try. Shall we do it? We can only do it together."

***

Nobody said a word except Mrs. Hurley as she stuffed another piece of cake into her mouth. "He must have overbalanced," she giggled. "Too much weight in his jacket pockets, most likely. D'you know, Mrs. Wells, I do like this cake! Did you make it yourself?"

If anybody had seen anything, nobody said a word. The police eventually wrote it off and some officers sighed with relief that the case was concluded as an accidental death.

Wragge's widow slipped quickly into a malaise of desperation when she found out how hated her husband had been. She found his money stashed away in safety deposit boxes in several banks. To make amends, she took up work in a charity shop and slipped a fifty-pound note into every item of recycled clothing in expiation of her husband's behaviour.

***

Everard had cleared only two of the many who fed off the misfortune of others. It was not enough to make a real difference. One thing was certain, though—he had made friends. Molly was treated with kindness wherever they went. Some people actually sought them out to give Molly treats. Everard was surprised when Joe Randolph, another bookie, vanished into thin air along with all his money. Could it have been that an example had been set?

It was at the beginning of April when Everard was arrested under the terrorism provisions granted to the police by the government. They questioned him for two days about what they called "an insurrection which threatened public security." He had no idea what they were talking about, but since the names of Dorkin and Wragge were never mentioned, he knew that he was not suspected of their deaths.

Mrs. Wells, on the other hand, had spread the word that Everard was being held at the local police station. That second night, the station's telecommunications system was knocked out along with all satellite phone coverage, and the building was demolished, brick by brick, by a furious crowd of those that society had turned its back on.

The police scattered in fear and confusion. They could not explain to themselves what had happened nor why they were targeted so unexpectedly. They had no idea that the seeds of a revolution had just been sown. The poor once again found it necessary to rebel. But this time, there was real organisation and determination to change everything that had favoured the rich to the detriment of the poor.

The dissent spread in total silence. None could foresee when the next assault might be nor from whence it might come. Racketeers vanished overnight, and where one police force was swept away, another type of force would take its place. But this time it was different. Coming from all sectors, these volunteers swept the detritus from the streets. It was no longer a safe place to be a loan shark in the poorer parts of North London, nor a pimp, a bookie, or a pusher of drugs. Bodies were rarely found and questions rarely asked as the rebellion slipped silently through the streets, drawing ever closer to the city and its institutions.

The number of participants increased over the next few years and with that came positive changes. Confiscated sums were shared around according to need and circumstance. Within days, committees were elected to organise the redistribution of assets. Rents were re-assessed taking into account the income or needs of the occupants. Empty properties were confiscated in order to house the homeless. The radical changes all happened so quickly. Within six weeks, much of North London was controlled by the people. Parliament slept on, unaware that the ground beneath their feet was moving inextricably away in a silence that only the dead would understand.

Everard looked at Molly. "What do you think, Molly?"

"Let's go round to see Mrs. Wells. She does a nice cup of tea and I do like the cake!' Molly grinned.

***

As they approached the stairs to Mrs. Wells's old apartment, their way was barred by two extremely ugly, black-suited oafs. One, who called himself "M" (Molly said it stood for mutt), was shaved, probably at all points, and had a neck wider than his ears. He stood around six feet six in height and picked his fingernails with the tip of his flick knife. His nose was as flat as his brain, having caught an iron bar in a pub brawl some years earlier.

His fellow, Tone, was twitchy. Not as brawny as M but equally as stupid, he wore a gardenia in his lapel. He thought that it gave him cachet, but instead, he just looked like a ponce. If Brylcreem needed support, he was there for it, his greasy locks stuck firmly to the back of his neck. Shaving was not his forte—one curly black hair proudly presented itself between the second and third buttons of his Domestos-bleached shirt. Blood stains? There were none.

"What?" said M threateningly.

"Stairs!" Everard replied.

"Who?" demanded Tone.

"None of your business," said Everard.

"What d'you mean, none of our business?"

"Exactly that. Since when do I have to explain myself and my business to a couple of morons like you two?"

"Since Mr. Honeylicker said so. And who are you calling morons?"

"Look, there's three of us altogether and my dog. My dog has a scientific degree in nasal identification and says that she can smell a moron at a hundred yards. She caught the whiff of you two as we entered the complex. So, it must be you. Now get out of the bloody way because I'm going upstairs whether you like it or not."

"You ain't going nowhere," said M, taking a step forward.

"Actually, you've just proved my point. It is, 'You aren't going anywhere.' You were right all along, Molly. They definitely are morons."

Everard shuffled around in his bag and produced the remains of a cheese sandwich. Tone thought it was a bomb and produced his favourite toy, a gold-plated 9mm Mauser, as did M, but his was more business-like and lacked the flashy ornamentation.

"Put the sandwich down! No quick moves. Real slow!" It was not a good move. Molly loved a cheese sandwich and made a swift grab before it touched the ground. Two shots rang out across the courtyard. Everard and Molly ran up the multitude of stairs as fast as their legs and paws could carry them to Mrs. Wells's apartment.

Everard remarked out of breath, "Oh, I'm so glad she's moving away. I don't think I could ever get used to this, Molly! I haven't a clue who's looking after us, but it certainly keeps us out of trouble, don't you think?" Everard sighed with a sort of ho-hum in his voice. Looking out the stairwell window, he and Molly were just in time to see a grey van disappear out of the courtyard with no sign of M nor Tone and no sign of their blood either.

"That was quick, wasn't it, Molly!"

Molly laughed.

***

The door to the apartment was open. Inside was Mr. Honeylicker seated on a wooden kitchen chair, his hands tied fast behind his back and a tight black cloth forcing his tongue back into his mouth. Mrs. Wells was feeding his nostrils with snuff.

"Hello, Everard! Hello, Molly! How's my Molly today?"

"Mrs. Wells! What on earth are you doing to him? He looks quite upset!"

"He'll feel a lot easier when I've finished, assuming, of course, that it has the same effect as when George, my husband, went. Too much snuff is not that good for you, can even be terminal. He sat there in that very chair, this same little tin in his hand when it happened. It was a new one he hadn't tried before— *Sid's Surprise*—that was the name on the tin. Anyway, he took a great sniff and then shouted, 'YES!' for all he was worth and sneezed.

"I tell you, Everard, it shouldn't have happened. Do you see the marks on the dresser there? That was where his teeth hit it. And then he said, 'Oh, my god!' and fell off the chair, stone dead, just like that. I said to Mr. Honeylicker here, 'Would you like to meet George, my husband?' and he said, 'Yes.' Then I said, 'Take a seat,' and he did, which gave me the chance to whack him with my rolling pin. Took him quite by surprise, it did. So then I had the chance to tie him up. By the way, my name is Doris, so forget about the Mrs. Wells stuff. After all, I am Molly's mum now, aren't I!"

Everard stood back for a moment to regard the unusual and courageous woman who stood before him. Wearing an apron with a printed portrait of Molly across the front, she had that look of determination blended with a touch of devilry.

"Mrs. Wells, Doris I mean, what are you going to do with him? He doesn't look too happy to me. I think he's had enough snuff. If he sneezes, he might explode, and that'll take you days to clear away the mess! Talking about mess, a couple of strange men confronted Molly and me at the foot of the stairway.

Somebody popped them off when they pulled their guns on me and Molly. But when we got to the top of the steps, they had gone, disappeared into thin air. What is going on? Are you going to tell me?"

"Oh, Everard, don't worry yourself about it. Just accept that it is the system now. Anyway, with this old fart, I thought I might starve him to death like he's treated some of his clients, but I think it would take too long, so then I thought I might try George's little tin. Oh, damn it! He's peed on my floor, the dirty sod!"

"I think we should have a discussion about this, don't you think? Take the gag off him and see what he's got to say for himself."

Everard couldn't stop himself from laughing. Doris undid the cloth and gave Honeylicker a hard shove at the back of his head. "Peeing on my floor, you bugger!" she chided.

Honeylicker coughed, leaving a trail of snuff-stained saliva trickling from the side of his floppy lips. Everard took the lead.

"What do you suggest we should do with you? By the way, your two friends have been removed, and you won't see them ever again. So any sensible suggestion from you may have an effect on whether you live or die. What's it to be, Mr. Honeylicker—life or death?"

Everard leaned forward to look directly into the fat, lumpy, over-fed face.

"You won't get away with this! You'll pay for this!"

"Wrong answer. Try again, Mr. Honeylicker."

"We'll get you, me and my boys. We'll have you and cut you up into little pieces!"

"Mr. Honeylicker, think about what I just said. Your boys are dead, gone, gone forever, okay?"

"What! M and Tone?"

"For Christ's sake, Mr. Honeylicker! How many more times do I have to tell you? They've gone! What is the matter with you? How on earth did you ever become whatever it is you are? Look at you! You've pissed yourself. You're at our mercy, if that's the word for it, and you're sitting there, tied up, and acting as if you haven't got a single brain cell. There's no answer for you, is there?

"Allow me to explain. Mrs. Wells is leaving this flat very soon, in a few hours in fact, and she won't be coming back. With the security deadlock on the door, nobody will try to get in for at least a month, and it will probably only be the flies that will eventually attract some attention. Do you understand more fully what your situation really is at this moment? I asked you, live or die. Give me a reply, one word."

"Live," croaked Honeylicker.

"So, what are you going to trade for your life?"

"Fifty thousand?"

"Is that all you think you're worth, a mere fifty thousand? Tut, tut, Mr. Honeylicker. To start with, we are going to take you home. We will set up our headquarters in your office, and your wife will make sure that you behave yourself."

"What do you mean, my wife? She's not in on this, is she?"

"She will be as soon as we get you home. Your and her options are very limited, you see. Your dirty little empire is finished. Isn't it, Doris?"

Doris had said nothing but had watched Everard with a fascination that brought more than a spark to her smile.

"Everard, come outside for a minute. I want to have a word."

Everard followed, wondering what Doris had in mind. From being a desolate old lady, facing life with little or no money, she had suddenly become a different person, much more positive and capable, but he had no idea of *how* capable.

"Everard, dear, as you say, Honeylicker lives in a house big enough for ten. You're right. We do need somewhere to work from, a kind of Government Communications HQ, if you see what I mean. He's bound to have a good phone and computer system to have run his racket for so long. But you must keep out of things. I know you started the uprising, for lack of a better word, but it has grown.

"You see, there are so many of us who became victims, thanks to the government and the greed of people like Honeylicker, and now the organisation runs itself. It has also given you a bodyguard. Whatever you do, keep your temper and keep out of the line of fire. Do this for Molly if nobody else and try to keep your nose clean.

"I take it that you saw the removal van from the top of the stairs. You are a dark one, aren't you! You didn't say a word about it! You obviously don't miss a thing, do you? I'll keep you in the picture as things change, but stay away from the organisation. Don't pry! There may be a thing or two that are necessary to do which you won't like.

"So now I'll leave it to you to get him ready to go home. I think he could be useful, so don't hurt him. I've got a couple of calls to make. There are some arrangements to sort out before we have supper tonight."

She winked at Molly and turning went away, out of sight, to somewhere in the maze of corridors and alleys that fringed the apartment block.

Everard returned to Honeylicker, not quite certain as to what he should say and certainly unsure as to how large the revolt that he had inadvertently started had grown.

Honeylicker was struggling to free himself but to no avail. Granny knots tied by Mrs. Wells were never going to be that easy to undo, basically due to their quantity. "Never use one when six will do" had always been a useful phrase for her. "Keeps your fingers nimble and your mind focused" was another.

Everard quietly leaned forward over Honeylicker's shoulder. "I suppose we need to talk now that things seem to be moving forward. I believe we might as well confiscate everything that you possess. You will continue to live at your present address and behave like a normal human being from now on. If you don't, then there will be sanctions. You will be allowed out to shop, but you will be watched, and any person that you contact may, depending on their circumstances and who they are, be eliminated.

"You're in the midst of a revolution. The best thing that you can do is to be nice. Do you understand? Your car, by the way, has just been commandeered. I saw it drive off as I came through the door, so it means you will have a rather long walk home, and with wet trousers, I'm afraid you'll get rather sore thighs with all that ammonia. Never mind. It's all part of the game."

Everard patted Honeylicker on the head and commenced to untie his hands.

"Up you get!"

Honeylicker staggered before stretching to his full six-feet-two height. He glowered down at Everard.

"Forget it, Honeylicker. You're being watched. Just behave yourself!"

***

Honeylicker was about fifty-five years old, had a waistline which necessitated the use of braces for his trousers, and in his case, he had chosen mauve leather. His shoes were handmade in two different sizes, the left foot being considerably shorter than the right, having lost a number of toes during another period of captivity. It was generally accepted that he had beaten his father to death during an argument over a pocket money rise when he was fourteen, which had set him on course to being a thorough nuisance to everyone around him.

He was not a happy man. Most of his days he spent being angry which, in turn, made him even more brutal. Moneylending was just a part of his self-employment. The rest consisted of his being just totally nasty. It was hard for him to take orders from a mere boy when a day earlier he would have laughed to see Everard torn apart by wild dogs. But that was his nature. He was going to have a really tough time.

The walk to his mansion was about four miles. Everard had spent a long time walking and was unbothered, but for Honeylicker, whose life was spent reclining in his limousine, it was a real hardship. It was even more galling for him to see his car in the drive as they arrived at the gates. Everard was also surprised and even more so when the front door opened, and there stood Mrs. Wells.

"Welcome home!" she said. "Mr. Honeylicker, you and your wife have got another bedroom now, the guest room. You have far too many gadgets in your old room that you might use to contact people that we don't want you to use. Okay?"

Honeylicker nodded and croaked, "Can I have shower now, and can I see my wife?"

"Yes, of course you can. Give her a shout. I think she'll be glad to see you. She's been crying a bit. I think she's a little frightened." Doris led the way inside the hallway as Mrs. Honeylicker appeared at the top of the wide stairway. She ran down and threw her arms around her husband.

Honeylicker sobbed, "They've killed Tone and M, Rachel. They were like sons to me."

"I know, darling. They brought them here in the car and buried them at the end of the lawn and planted some roses on top of them. Considerate, really, bearing in mind that they were dead."

"What on earth are you talking about? They are the ones that killed them! They are dead! My two boys are dead!"

"Yes, I know, dear. But they're such lovely roses, and they did bring the boys home, didn't they? They could have left them in a skip or something. You would have done that, wouldn't you?"

"Are you going soft or what?" Honeylicker pushed Rachel away. "Have they been getting at you?" he shouted.

"No ... well, just a bit. They're only trying to help people to have a better life. A lot of what they said was nice—how they want to help the elderly and help youngsters find work. They're really very nice, you know."

Honeylicker was becoming red at the ears. "Rachel, these are the people that we've been living off of for the past three years. These people owe us a great deal of money. I can see there's no chance of getting it back now. In fact, I've been told by this idiot here that we've lost everything, house an' all."

"We'll be alright, luv. Don't worry." She looked over to Everard. "We will be alright, won't we?"

Everard smiled as Rachel led Honeylicker upstairs to where she tried in vain to comfort her husband through the shower room door.

***

Up to that point, Everard had not seen any sign of a conspiracy or revolutionary council. Mrs. Wells ... Doris ... was the only person visible in the revolt. As he walked back with Honeylicker, not a soul had shown itself in the hour and a half that it took to get back. The streets had been deserted, which was odd for that time of day.

"Doris, where are the others?" he asked.

"Oh, they're around. Don't worry, Everard. It's just that we don't want you to have any trouble, just as I said earlier. Where's my Molly, then? Come on! Let's have some tea! We'll have it in the sitting room."

The room was large with a good view of the garden. Rachel had gone down and was already watering the roses that had been planted. A computer screen on a desk in the corner showed that somebody had been busy. Page laid upon page of bank accounts were clearly visible. A ballpoint with the cap still off rested on a sheet of calculations. Everard felt the seat. It was still warm.

Nothing seemed right anymore, and he wondered whether he had just been caught up in a dream. He could see Rachel talking to somebody out of sight behind a hedge.

Doris returned with a tray laden with fruitcake and three cups of tea.

"Here we are, Molly! Do you realise, Everard, if it hadn't been for Molly, none of this would've happened. I suppose that I should tell you precisely how far things have gone. It's quite surprising really. We have cleared every loan shark out of the whole of North London, as far out as the M25. Not only that, but we have also taken control of the prisons on this side, and parliament is still so busy messing around with electioneering that they haven't even noticed the change.

"We gave the police a chance — join us or become unemployed. Very few chose the second option, and a few took transfers to other parts or early retirement. However, there were some, quite a lot in fact, who we knew had over-policed at demonstrations to protect the so-called greater democracy and who are now serving time at our pleasure, so they are out of the picture.

"The beauty is that we now have solidarity. There are thousands and thousands who are with us, and not a word is uttered to the other authorities. We have set up work units with proper wages and commandeered factories. The old ruling class has fallen away without a word, and it all seems to be working out quite well. We expect some kind of backlash, but nothing has taken shape yet, and the longer it goes on the way it has, then eventually it will be too late for a reprisal, provided that all continues to succeed.

"The next step is to declare North London a separate state and declare our independence. There's a lot to think about though. We are trying to keep it as bloodless as possible, but I'm sure that there will be some casualties, particularly among the rich."

Chapter 2

Wednesday morning was a wet one. The rain was not heavy but was sufficiently cold to make life uncomfortable. The House of Commons was almost empty. Poverty was never a concern for most politicians unless they had fallen over a starving child on the doorstep of No.10. So when Richard Bartroot, the Home Secretary, received an unexpected phone call from his old friend and colleague, Cyril Hogpart, he was a little perplexed. It was a simple two-word call. The voice cried out, "Help me," before the line went dead. Bartroot was not used to helping people and saw himself in a real dilemma. Why should he help Hogpart? After all, he was only a friend.

"Oh, forget it! It's only Hogpart. He was bound to come a cropper sooner or later."

Hogpart had been curb-crawling outside a school early that morning, looking for a pick-up with anyone under sixteen, male or female, who might satisfy him for twenty quid. He had visited most schools around London at one time or another during the past years that he had been an MP. If ever he was challenged, he would simply declare himself as an honourable member looking after the interests of the educational system and making certain that the children were safe in the vicinity of the schools or their playgrounds. It had always worked before, but this time was different. The evidence started coming in.

"Miss, it was him who did my brother and sister. I saw them get in his car, and when they came back that night, a social worker came by and took them away. She said that they'd been abused by my parents. But it's not true, Miss. They never did anything nasty to them, and it's not fair because we don't know where they are. What's worse is that the Social denies any knowledge of them. Are they lying, Miss?"

Hogpart was in big trouble, but to trace the children and all the others who had vanished in various locations gave the revolutionary judges a problem. It was necessary to make an example of Hogpart, to make him suffer publicly, but to do it then would mean the silence and the secrecy of the new society would be broken. Was it ready to reveal itself or did it need more time? To keep Hogpart under wraps would have lengthened the time that the missing children would suffer. It had to be now. There was no other option.

There was a lot of work to be done in East London. The criminal element was much more organised and harder to destroy. Several members of the Revolutionary Police were killed in shootouts with the drug gangs, and the fallout was having a bad effect on the general morale.

"Everard, my dear, it had to happen, didn't it? Without an all-out war in the East End, how are we going to reach out further? People there are frightened of retaliation if they talk to us. Have you got any suggestions? And then there's Hogpart. What about him?"

"Doris, the problem is that the two are unrelated. We need to look at history to examine what a revolution has to do to succeed. Firstly, do we want the public to be our friends, or do we want to keep them in order with terror tactics? The French revolution succeeded because it had the guillotine and punished the old system adherents by removing heads. France is still a republic. But then look at ISIS. They are using terror to subjugate anybody who refuses to join them or is of the wrong class or religion. They are bound to fail in the end.

"We have to be selective to gain strong support. The East End gangsters need to be captured, paraded and executed, their assets seized and returned to pay for local development, you know, playgrounds for the kids, music halls and karaoke bars for the older people, theatres and sport centres, all free. Then we will have friends. But Hogpart, he's different. What would you do, Doris?"

"I'd have him stripped, tattooed with all his crimes listed on his chest, and tied to a post in Parliament Square until he gave up all the names of his accomplices and the whereabouts of all the children that have gone missing because of him."

"Well, that's a good start, and I go along with the main idea, but Parliament Square? It would bring too much of the government's attention to what you and the rest are doing.

"Doris, I know what you said to me earlier, and I accept the principle of the argument, but I have to ask. How accessible is the council, the revolutionary council? I have not seen anybody in the last months, only changes with nobody visible causing them. It's brilliant, but how do I speak to somebody if I have a need to report something and that sort of thing?

"Now that everything has reached this point, it could be time to challenge the validity of the government. The politicians seem only interested in following their own programs without any reference to the public. It appears that once they're elected, everything else no longer matters. So how about the general council showing themselves to the public, explaining the course of action that they have taken, what their plans are, and then confronting the government with a mandate from our people?"

Doris listened attentively as Everard spoke. She was proud of how far he'd come in the last two years, but at twenty-six, he still had much to learn. "Everard, my dear, you can be so naive. It's just not the right time. I agree that the public should see us and know the good that has been achieved. Let them hear from the residents in the section that we now control. Then we will quietly gain support until we can literally overthrow the government. We need to gain that support, and to do that, we need to enlarge the area which we control. It'll take a while yet, but I'm sure we can do it."

"You're probably right, Doris, but what about Hogpart? He should be put on trial, but we need to know who he's with. Do we force it out of him?"

"My mum used to get my dad drunk when she wanted to know the truth. She knew that he had a weak threshold and could never sustain any kind of pressure when he was tipsy, and with another couple of drinks inside him, he would blurt out any number of secrets. In Hogpart's case, I think he needs to be assessed. If drink worked on my dad, then maybe Hogpart will tell all. My mum used to make plum brandy in the old wash boiler she kept in the outside lattie, only for medicinal purposes, you understand. But it was as good as a lie detector when she suspected something."

"Doris, Doris, Doris. Who is actually running things? Look, I started it, or so it seems, and I haven't a clue as to what's going on now. Is there a revolutionary council or not? Someone I can speak to? Is there actually *a* council? Any kind of council? I know you say there is, and if that is so, I want to meet someone. Doris, I have to know. Get me a rendezvous. Hogpart has got my blood up, and I want to get those kids back. Okay?"

"Everard, dear, I need to go. Come back tomorrow at around 11 a.m. and I'll try to get something sorted out, somebody to talk to, alright? Do you want to leave Molly here for the night? She's more than welcome."

"What do you say, Molly? Your choice."

"Is it beans, potatoes, and dog biscuits?" Molly replied. Doris nodded.

"Okay, then. I'll stay." Molly jumped up onto a chair at the dining table and pulled a placemat towards her with her left paw.

Everard laughed and made for the door.

"Don't you want some as well?" Doris called out.

"Sounds tempting, but no. I'll see you at eleven."

***

Everard took a cab to the eastern edge of the newly civilised zone. As he passed by the main streets of the sector, he could see that people looked more relaxed, many sitting in the evening sun outside bars and pubs despite the cool breeze, with no sign of anxiety or mistrust. It didn't appear normal, but there it was, quite real.

The cab driver, an Albanian, explained that it was not safe for him to go further into East London since he had no licence to operate in those parts. He told Everard that he would need to pay and register with so many gangs just to pass through and he would never have the money to get back again. Everard felt his blood rising once more. Something had to be done.

The last thing one might expect to see is a roadblock in London, least of all one guarded by heavily armed police. Whose police, though? Of course, they were the new formation and stopped any suspicious traffic from entering the new civilisation. The tariffs imposed by the East London gangs had more or less stifled any movement of goods in either direction, and for the time being, there was little or no aggression.

The driver stopped his cab, "Look, mate, I think you're bolder than you look, but this is as far as I can go if I want to live. So give us a fiver, and I wish you all the best with whatever you are up to. Good luck, mate!"

As he stood at the side of the road, Everard could see there was barely a chance of success in a straightforward invasion, but a subtle house by house, street by street infiltration would be the only way to expand into new territory. But one thing bothered him ... did the residents of East London actually want to be social, friendly and dare he think it ... happy? It was a dilemma, but it had to be considered. He leaned against a tree and sighed to himself. *What can I do?*

***

Children are vulnerable to predators, but despite that, they can be very manipulative and extremely resilient. Everard could hear the caustic cacophony of their laughter distantly. Maybe the answer lay there. Following the cries of a child, he soon found what could be considered an excuse for a playground: two of the three swings vandalised, the roundabout off its centre spindle, and the see-saw sawn through.

As he approached the playground, he was hardly noticed. He leisurely chose a bench and sat down with legs outstretched. It was not long before he was approached by a rather tanned, scrawny, dark-eyed boy, about twelve or thirteen years old.

As he neared Everard, he scuffed his shoes on the grass at the side of the pathway as if to remove something that a dog had left behind. He searched around in his pocket and produced a very bent and somewhat crushed hand-rolled cigarette. Sitting about three feet away from Everard on the bench, he casually leaned in Everard's direction.

"Got a light, mister?"

"Sorry, mate. I gave it up when I was ten. Mugs game, smoking. Makes your skin turn grey, just like yours."

"What d'yer mean? I look like that, do I? My mums been smokin' ever since my brother got killed a few years ago. She never stops, lights up all the time, but she's not grey. Bit red but that's probably the drink. That's why I took it up, to keep her company, if you know what I mean. I don't like the booze though. Makes me feel really sick. What are you doing here, anyway? You're not one of them, are you? You don't look like one anyway. Have you got any money?"

Everard thought at that moment that there could be a way into the boy's confidence. "Yeah, I've got some money. Much more than I used to have. Why do you want to know?"

"Are you going to offer me some?" the boy quickly responded.

"No! And why should I?"

"Just checking you out. So why are you here? People don't come here on the off chance. They're sent. So who sent you?"

"Nobody sent me. I came here for a reason, but I'm not sure about you, whether I can trust you or not."

The reply was exactly what Everard had hoped for. "Bloody hell, mate! What do you take me for? I'm no runner for no one. Not anymore."

Everard wasted no time, knowing that a truthful account was to follow. He looked very seriously at the boy. "How did your brother get killed? Was it an accident?"

"No. He was hit by a lorry when he was racing his BMX down Mosely Road. Not like her, though!" The boy pointed to a young girl, probably about ten years old, dressed in her Sunday best but standing alone with loneliness stamped right across her little face.

"Her brother got knifed when he was running an errand for the old dear in the sweet shop over the road. You know, she's the word for the big nobs. They tell her what they want, and she sees to it. Gets the kids to run for them, and she gives them sweets or fags in payment. I've done a bit for her myself, but sod the fags. Besides, I don't eat sweets no more. I found out what I was carrying, and I tell you what. It was bloody bad news. Little bags of white powder, and my mum said it weren't flour. Too dangerous what with all the killings round here."

Everard thought for a moment. "Does the little girl know who killed her brother?"

"Course she does! We all do. Well, most of us. What's it to you, anyway? You're not the cops, are you?"

"No chance!" Everard replied, "But do you like the way it is round here, you know, the gangsters and all?"

"What! When we all have to watch our step otherwise Mum or Dad will get done over if we don't do as we're told? I can't wait to get away from here when I'm older. Problem is it takes money to do anything, and my mum says that it's those bastards who take it before anybody has a chance to spend it on anything. Just look at the clothes that girl's wearing. She got nothing else to put on. That's her compensation for losing her brother, and they were really close, you know."

"Look, mate," Everard suggested, "you seem pretty pissed off with what's going on. It seems to me that there are certain people around here who need to be taken out of the picture. What do you think? Are you interested in giving me and an old lady I know a bit more information, like who these people are and maybe where we can meet them? My old friend is very good at sorting things out for the good. She's a bit of a laugh as well, and she doesn't eat sweets nor smoke neither. Remember, smoking's a mugs game!"

"Yeah, I'll go along with that. I'm in here most days. Don't like school too much. By the way, you see that old geezer over there? He's one of them, watches us every day. He's even got a camera that he keeps hidden in his coat. If you look away for an instant, he takes a snap. But it's what he gets out of it which is crap. He gets photos of dead people, people that the Pyles brothers have done away with, and that old bastard shows the youngsters here, and it terrifies them. I've seen them, those photos. The bastards! That old shit tells the kids that their mums and dads will get the same if they don't do what they're told, and you know what that means. Yeah, I'll help you. I'm bloody sick of it all!"

Everard was hopeful. Having a possible ally in the area would give him more room to manoeuvre. "Give me a couple of days and I'll see what I can sort out. How do your parents feel about everything? What if they needed to go somewhere safe and quickly. Would they go? How can we contact them? Is there a phone number or something?"

"Don't know if they would go or not. They moan a lot, but they were brought up here and all their friends are here, so I don't know if they would take the chance. What they would need is something to really scare them. Why don't you go and give that old bastard over there a bit of a roughin' up? I'll tell you what. If you do that, the Pyles brothers will go round to my house and put the shits up my mum and dad. I won't go home tonight."

The lad continued. "I'll try to make it out of the East End and get to Muswell Hill without being seen. Do you know where that is? I went there once. There's a roundabout where the buses go. If I can make it without getting caught, I'll see you there at midday tomorrow. See yer! Kick him in the balls, that'll do it. And nick his camera. You'll see what he's got on it then! Have you got a pen?"

Richie scribbled something on the back of a discarded envelope. "Look, here's the telephone number. Give them a call roundabout eleven tonight, just before they go to bed. By the way, my name's Richie. What's yours?" The youngster had slipped Everard the telephone number of his parents as he got up to leave.

"My name's Everard, Richie. I'll see you tomorrow if all goes well. Take care, won't you? There's a lot that can happen between now and then, so just watch out."

Everard watched him go, and when he felt the youngster was safely out of the way, he strolled aimlessly over to the bench where the creepy older man was sitting. He carefully brushed the seat meaningfully before sitting down.

"You never know what's been sitting here before you, do you? Do you ever sit on this side ever?" Everard teased the start of a conversation.

"Why? What's it to you? I've been watching you, and I'll tell you now. You better watch yerself when you come sniffin' round here."

"Why's that then? Are you some kind of clever clogs who takes care of things, or are you just some paltry shit that sticks to the shoes of your bosses?"

"You'd better shut your mouth, mate, before I put the word out!"

Everard smiled. "And how are you going to do that, then?"

It was so quick, the older guy didn't see it coming. With a sudden, sharp jab, Everard jerked his elbow hard into the other man's face, scoring a direct hit on his nose, which responded with a nasty crunch. The man fell back, blood streaming from his broken nose. Everard took the camera from the inside pocket of the man's raincoat, took a photo of his victim, and sauntered off as if nothing had taken place. He crossed the road to the sweet shop.

"Look at this!" he said to the old lady. "What do you think?"

"Did you do that? Here, that's his camera you're holding … you, you … bastard!" Everard turned and walked out of the shop.

***

It was something of a surprise the following morning when Doris held her newspaper out to Everard as they sat chatting about the preceding day's events and how to bring the young lad into the safety of her flat.

"You did say that you elbowed him on the nose, didn't you? Funny, because here it says that you smashed his head in with a club hammer, breaking the whole of the front of his face. I think that he must have become the victim of his own malevolence. They certainly know how to build on a story, don't they? Let's face it. What use is he to them now that his usefulness has come to an end? We really need to pick your young friend up very, very quickly. Those Pyles brothers are definitely not very nice. The sooner we deal with them, the better."

Everard sat quietly, deep in thought for some time but eventually suggested, "What would you think if I went back to the sweet shop and told the woman that I'm taking over and that from now on she will be working for me?"

"There are two words for that, Everard. One starts with *F* and the other is stupid! You wouldn't last five minutes, and I don't want to lose you and neither does Molly. Just think of that! We'll sort it out. Don't you worry about that. But we have to deal with the local police first. There will have to be a real clear out, that's for sure.

"There's only one way people like that can flourish and that is with the connivance of some of the coppers. It strikes me that there are a lot of them growing fat on turning a blind eye.

"Look, I'm going to make a couple of calls in a minute, and with a bit of luck, we'll have your little mate's folks somewhere safe as soon as we get their agreement. They said that they would like to think about it last night, but I believe that they were under a lot of duress, if you see what I mean. I just hope that nothing too drastic has happened to them since then. It's going to be tricky getting them out without being seen and the only way will be to give the Pyles brothers' heavies a bit of a surprise ... make them aware of their own vulnerability. It's always so amusing because, for a lot of them, it will be the first time that they will have felt any fear. It's just a shame that after they get their just desserts, they will have never had the chance to change their ways."

Everard looked sideways at Doris and thought to himself, *Is this really the same old lady I saw in the pension queue?*

Chapter 3

Everard waited in the doorway of a shop with an easy view of the roundabout at Muswell Hill from midday to one o'clock. He had clothed himself in a dark blue raincoat and scribbled aimlessly on a sheet of paper clipped to the top of a rectangular piece of hardboard. Every time a bus passed, he looked at his watch and noted the time of its arrival. Nobody questioned his activity or lack of it, assuming that he was part of the system checking on the punctuality of the bus service, but the lad failed to show himself. There was, however, a young woman who seemed very anxious and who appeared at regular intervals during his observations to be waiting for some kind of connection. Everard took the chance and approached her in a somewhat casual manner.

"Can I help you, miss? You seem to be looking for your bus connection."

"No, I don't want a bus. I need to get back to work, but I was given a message to deliver to somebody who would be here at midday. But nobody seems to be waiting, or at least I haven't seen anyone."

"Is it a message regarding a young lad around twelve years old?"

"Why, yes! How would you know that?"

"Because I've been waiting for him to show since 12 o'clock. What's happened to him?"

"Oh," she said, "Do you know him? Are you related?"

"Yes, I'm his uncle," Everard lied. Telling the young woman that Richie was his friend would probably sound suspicious, and he wanted to hear whatever information she had about him.

She came closer and said in a low tone, "He's in the burn unit at the Royal Free. It's not really that bad, but it's not good. He was picked up last night by a taxi driver. Apparently, he was being chased down the road by some men, and his shirt was on fire. Look, here's the note. I think he wants you to visit. God, look at the time! I'm sorry, I've got to get back to the hospital or I'll get the sack."

Everard watched her disappear just as the rain started to fall. *Hmm, good thing I've got this raincoat,* he thought to himself, and raising his hand, he hailed a taxi.

It was an awkward situation. As the torrential rain poured, Everard noticed that he was not the only one needing a lift. A woman, more ancient than many and clutching two large carrier bags, hailed the same cab. As Everard opened the taxi door to climb in, he was surprised to be pushed aside with a smile.

"Thank you, young man. That's so kind of you. Can I give you a lift? Are you going in the same direction as I am? We can share the fare if you like."

Everard stuck his head through the cab driver's door. "Royal Free ... emergency. I'll sort it out with the lady. Oh, also there's a young woman in a yellow coat walking quickly down that road there. Pick her up as we go, if you will."

The taxi driver obliged, but the old lady thought that she was being kidnapped, and after being joined by the young woman, she became even more convinced.

"What are you going to do with me? I don't want to go to hospital. There's nothing wrong with me! I'm just old, that's all! Don't touch me ... you, you ... terrorist!"

Sarah, the young woman in the yellow coat, calmed the old lady and explained that there was an emergency, and she was not being kidnapped. Everard said nothing but bit his lip several times as he tried to figure out the next move.

Sarah tried to calm the agitated woman. "Don't worry. Once we reach the hospital, this young man will help you get to your destination, but for the moment, we need to make sure that a young lad is safe."

"So why have I been kidnapped? I don't know the young lad!"

"No, you haven't been kidnapped. It's just that the taxi was needed to get us to the hospital."

"So why am I here if I haven't been kidnapped? That's what I want to know!"

Everard responded, "Because you got into the taxi that I had flagged down as soon as I opened the door! You just happened to invite yourself into this dilemma." Everard had obviously gotten tired of the cantankerous old lady. "And now just be quiet while I try to think!"

A few minutes later, the cab arrived at the Royal Free. Sarah waited as Everard asked the old woman where she wanted to go so that he could pay for her return fare.

"I want to go to the roundabout at Muswell Hill. Thank you."

"Why do you want to go there?" Everard was truly perplexed.

"Well, that's where I live. Just down the road in Colney Hatch. It's only a couple of paces from the roundabout."

"Then why did you get in this taxi?"

"Well ... you held the door open for me."

Everard banged his head on the roof of the cab and gave the driver a twenty-pound note.

"Take her back, will you?"

Sarah pulled his arm to extricate him from his mounting dilemma. "Quick," she said, "We've got to go!"

***

At the hospital, Sarah led Everard to the lift that would take them to Richie's private room.

"I don't think we've been properly introduced. I'm Sarah," she said as she extended her hand, smiling timidly.

"I'm Everard. Very pleased to meet you, Sarah," he replied in a daze. *She's so beautiful.*

Their hands touched for a second too long, their eyes locked in an intense gaze, broken only when the elevator bell pinged as they reached their floor.

The rain had dampened her chestnut-brown hair which hung in dripping rivulets around her face. Her unblemished complexion had a touch of blush pink on her cheeks and lips, bringing out the softness of her amber eyes. She wasn't very tall, perhaps five feet five, and was certainly well-proportioned, visible even in her loose-fitting uniform. Everard hoped to get to know her better.

Entering Richie's room, he was surprised to see Mrs. Wells sitting on a chair next to the boy's bed.

"Hello Everard! Where have you been? Richie thought you must have got caught by the thugs who did this to him."

Sarah fussed around Richie's bed for a few minutes and then slipped away.

"Back in a while," she said, giving Everard a curious glance as she went. Everard did not miss it. He thought, *What was that all about?*

"Now, how the hell did you get into this state, Richie? Who did this to you, or do I have to ask? And what about your parents? Do they know you're here?"

Richie groaned. He was lying flat on his stomach, the burns being for the most part along the top of his back which was badly scorched as was the back of his scalp. "Tell him, will you, Mrs. Wells! I can't go through it all again!"

"Everard, listen. This is what happened. After you left, the bloke at the playground told the brothers about your visit and what you did to him. He took them round to Richie's parents' house where they waited for Richie to come home. They had broken the door open to get in and beat up Richie's mum and dad and locked them in the upstairs back bedroom. But Richie always went home the back way, through a gap in the garage-block wall.

"His mum spotted him as he returned and tried to warn him. As it happened, one of the brothers had gone to the kitchen at the back of the house and saw Richie leaving the garden and gave chase. Richie had only gone back to check on his parents' welfare. However, another kid, one of the brothers' minions, saw Richie coming away as fast as he could run and tripped him up, basically only to gain favour with the brothers, and Richie was grabbed and carried off to an empty warehouse in Rees-Mogg Lane.

"Richie told them that all he did was to ask you for a light and then he told them that you saw the old man watching and whacked him on the nose for being nosey. That was all he said, and they replied, 'You wanted a light, did you?' Then they squirted a bottle of lighter fuel over him and threw a match towards him. Richie made a run for it and thought that the match had missed him, but then he realised that his shirt was on fire, and he kept on running while trying to get it off.

"It was a taxi driver who saved him, ripped the shirt off, threw Richie into the back of his cab, and drove off as fast as he could because he could see the two thugs quite close and gaining on Richie. Then he brought Richie here to the hospital. Here's his card. He's worth talking to and quite brave if you get my drift. Then they finished what you started with the old guy, just like that!"

Everard leaned close to Richie. "Well Richie, you were lucky to get away, weren't you, mate? Look, I'm really worried about your folks, and it's now going to be really difficult to get them out. Those Pyles brothers seem to like to hurt people, so I think they should be repaid in kind. How much property do they own in your area, preferably vacant or only used by themselves? Do you know? Also, is there some place that is important enough to distract them from looking at your parents? We can then get your mum and dad away quickly. But, Richie, we haven't got much time to play with. So what do you think? Anything spring to mind?"

"Look, mate, not so much pressure on the sheet if you don't mind. I'm a bit sore and the heat makes it feel worse."

"Oh, sorry, Richie," he said as he quickly stood.

"Yeah, there is a place. It's in an empty building, number 13 Johnson Street. There's a big place downstairs where they gamble, you know poker and things. They take girls there sometimes and young women from outside England, Latvia or something. I don't know much about geography. I had to take some stuff there once, and it stinks down there, you know, old perfume, dirty old men and filthy bedding … not nice at all.

"But the thing is, I spotted a safe in one of the rooms where one of the brothers was. That's on the left, third door along a corridor at the back of the main room. Now if you could wreck that place, then they would definitely forget my mum and dad for a couple of days. That's the best place I can think of at the moment."

"Is there much activity there, do you know?" Everard asked.

"Mainly at weekends but sometimes on Thursdays. I think they use it then for planning or plotting — whatever it's called — and maybe counting their money. All I know is that you can't park a car there on that day because the street's full of limos. Greasy bastards!" Richie gave a small cough and grimaced. "This is really sore, you know. I hope you get them or do something really nasty to pay them back for me."

Everard was about to pat Richie's shoulder when he remembered that it would not be appreciated. It was at that moment that Sarah returned.

"I'm sorry, you two, but it's time to change his dressings, and besides that, he needs to rest. There's a man downstairs claiming to be a detective, asking if a youngster with burns has been brought in. I don't think he's real, and I told the receptionist to say that Richie has been sent home. I hope that's okay."

Everard looked at Sarah with a mixture of curiosity and admiration and thought to himself, *Sarah is certainly resourceful, and I think she could be a good friend to us.* Turning to Richie, "Looks like they want you dead, young man. I think we need to do something about that, don't we?"

Chapter 4

Mrs. Wells made her excuses to Everard by claiming that she needed to pick up some dog food for Molly. "I'll see you at around four at my place and we'll have a chat and some dinner. I'm sure Molly would like to see you if only for you to take her for a walk."

It was a rebuke of sorts since Everard had somewhat neglected his dog over the preceding days. The problem was Molly was comfortable with Mrs. Wells—regular meals, strolling in the park, and television to watch. It was a lot better than life on the streets. As for Everard, he missed that life, strange as it may seem. He missed the coming and going of the rush hour, the congress of the world blindly passing him by, day after day, seemingly as aimless as was his life. But there was one glimmer of hope in his mind … Sarah. He found himself thinking about her more and more.

Everard arrived almost at the appointed time, three minutes past four. Mrs. Wells met him at the door and handed him Molly's lead with the dog attached.

"There you are, Molly! Everard is going to take you for a nice walk. Aren't you, my dear!"

Everard looked down at Molly. She was so excited. Her face was full of it. And it worked. Everard smiled. "Okay you! Come on then. Let's go!" Everard needed to do it. He was losing sight of who he was before his world had suddenly changed, but half an hour with Molly found him sitting on a bench with her sitting beside him with his arm around her neck.

"Bit like old times, isn't it?" Molly whispered as she licked his cheek.

"I'm sorry, Molly. I really have neglected you, haven't I?"

She stopped licking him for a moment and sniffed around his armpit.

"Everard! You're wearing a deodorant. Something's changed! Is it me or are you looking for love?"

"You never miss a thing, do you Molly!"

"Well, I *am* a dog!"

***

When they got back to Mrs. Wells's apartment, she greeted them with a smile and a single word: "Sorted!"

"Doris, not again. What have you sorted, or need I ask?"

"I thought it was a good idea to move the situation on as quickly as possible, so I phoned Joe who has a skip business in Eltham, and he agreed just like that!"

"Doris, what have you arranged? For a start, I don't believe in this Joe with a skip business. I know you won't tell me who you've really spoken to, so come out with it. What has been arranged?"

"Everard, look. I spoke to—you know—the one you don't know, and we agreed that a skip full of slaughterhouse junk, the stuff that not even the dogmeat place can use, emptied on the steps and door of the club that Richie mentioned will definitely divert those thugs' attention. And I'll tell you something. Nobody, but nobody will want to go anywhere near that place for a good few weeks."

"So when is this going to happen, Doris? You have that look. Don't tell me."

"Well, I think it's already done, and I'm just waiting for a call letting me know that Richie's mum and dad are at the hospital with their son."

A few minutes later, Mrs. Wells received the call she had been waiting for.

"All done!" she declared triumphantly as she hung up the receiver. "All sorted! If you'd like to stay for dinner, you'll have a chance to meet them, that's if you want to. They'll be staying here for a while and moving on to a quiet location in about a week. We have annexed the kiddies' play area and taken over the sweet shop. The old girl who ran the place didn't want to go, but I think she's now cruising down the Thames on a biscuit, and we all know what happens to biscuits when they get wet!"

Everard mused over the time since he first put an end to the old regime at the post office and wondered what he had unleashed. He looked at Doris. She was no longer the sixty-five-year-old, demoralised, sad old lady who he had reimbursed. She was now somebody he no longer knew. She had become ruthless though not ambitious, somebody who considered that action was more important than persuasion. She was now the secret empress of a domain and not shy of piracy to achieve the desired outcome of the events that Everard himself had created.

Snobby Pyles and his brother, Pikey, were doomed to lose their grip along with the spies and minions that held their little empire together, that was for sure.

Everard looked at her and was surprised to see, for the first time, a strange, pale purple light emanating from her. Even as she spoke, it appeared to puff out as a thin mist surrounding her. Everard pinched the skin over his stomach and muttered to himself, *I'm not seeing this. This is not real!*

"Yes, Doris. I will stay for dinner if only to keep Molly company." He laughed but gave Doris an odd look as she looked away. *Of course it wasn't true ... Nothing there now!*

As Doris turned to face him, she commented in surprise, "Everard, you look like you've seen a ghost! What's wrong?" It was said with twinkle in her eye.

Everard became even more confused, but at that moment, the doorbell rang.

"Would you answer that for me, Everard? I need to go to the loo." Doris quickly slipped out of the room. Molly was already at the door, tail wagging, excitedly looking back at Everard.

"Quick, quick, open it, open it!" she barked, her tail wagging excitedly.

Everard looked down at her. "What if I don't? What if I just go back to the couch and ignore the door?"

"Then you're a bloody fool! It will be your dumbest mistake!" Molly thought about biting him, but she didn't. "For god's sake, open the bloody door!" Molly had never spoken to him like that before, and Everard felt somewhat undermined.

As he opened the door, Doris called out from the lounge, "Come in, Sarah. I'm glad you could find us!" Everard blushed, stood aside and pressed himself against the wall as Sarah passed in front of him.

He looked at her surprised, unable to speak.

"Everard, are you alright? You look a little flushed. Have you got a temperature?" Sarah put her hand on his forehead as Everard tried not to wilt. It was not that Everard was shy or that he had never had any contact with the opposite sex. It was simply that he was fundamentally unprepared for the situation. Of course, Sarah knew all this. She could see it as if it was written in thick black ink across his brow.

Sarah felt unquestionably attracted to him. There was a mystique about him as indefinable as his spartan black attire. But there was a gentle softness in his big brown eyes, made even more appealing by his unusually long lashes. He was mesmerizing! What lay beyond that veil of innocence? What had those eyes seen?

She took his hand and led him into the lounge where Doris was trying to suppress her amusement.

"Everard, would you like to offer Sarah a drink? There's a selection of wine on the dresser and glasses in the cupboard below, and I'll have one of the reds, if you will."

Everard stumbled on the way to the dresser, filled a glass for Doris, and turned to Sarah.

"I'll have whatever you're having," she said.

"I think I'll try some of Doris's Corbière red. I hear it's an excellent wine. Want to try some?"

"Yes, that'd be lovely. Thank you."

His hand noticeably shook as he brought the glass to Sarah, spilling a bit on Doris's expensive Persian rug. Dammit! I hope she doesn't notice.

Once again, the doorbell rang. Everard jumped up immediately to answer. Two figures stood before him, both pale.

"Is this the home of Mrs. Wells?" the woman asked.

"Everard, let them in. It's Richie's folks."

Everard greeted them cordially and ushered the couple into the lounge as Doris did her best to make them feel welcomed. Sarah had already met them as Richie's nurse and expressed her pleasure to see them again.

Doris ushered Mr. and Mrs. Blake into the guest bedroom and showed them where to stow away the contents of their hurriedly packed suitcases. When they had finished, they returned to the lounge.

"How do you two feel about leaving the East End?" Everard asked.

"We would have preferred to stay, but it's become too dangerous after what happened to Richie. Those brothers need to be got rid of before they hurt any more people. By the way, we really appreciate what all of you have done for Richie and us. We don't want to be any trouble, but it seems at the moment that there is no end to our problems. By the way, I am Lyn and this is Alan, Richie's dad."

Everard realized he hadn't spoken with Richie since his visit to the hospital. "How was Richie this afternoon when you saw him? Is he doing okay? I would have gone back to check on him, but something came up and slightly derailed my plans."

Lyn replied, "He's been healing well, ready to be discharged soon, I would imagine. He'd like to see you again, Everard. I gathered he's gotten quite close to you. Richie's just turning fifteen, you know, and has always had a mind of his own. He's too independent for his own good, but he's mature beyond his years and quite savvy. Alan and I have had such a tough time keeping tabs on him, and as a mother, I worry so about him. But so far he's managed to keep himself out of trouble until now. He told us that he's also glad that we are now outside that area. As for those evil brothers, well, we could tell you a thing or two about them, couldn't we, Alan?" Richie's dad nodded vigorously and raised his eyes to the heavens.

"And on that happy note, let's eat!" Doris announced. She had kept busy in the kitchen warming up dinner and setting the dining table with Sarah's help while Everard learned as much as he could from the Blakes. It was a simple dinner of shepherd's pie served with garlic butter mushrooms, glazed carrots, and sourdough bread.

"Everard, I know you're a vegetarian, so help yourself to as much as you like from the salad bowl. Oh, Molly, you're dribbling all over my rug. Here you are," she said, spooning a heaping serving of shepherd's pie into her bowl.

"You're a vegetarian?" Sarah commented. "So am I!"

"Well, fancy that!"

The animated conversation turned to diet choices followed by a mélange of trivial topics and humorous stories, a welcomed reprieve from the usual talk of politics and murderous shysters.

Afterwards, the friendly exchange carried on in the lounge until Lyn glimpsed at her watch and said, "Oh, my, it's getting a bit late and we have much to do tomorrow, so I think Alan and I will retire for the evening. Thank you for a lovely evening, Doris. Everard, it was lovely meeting you, and I'm sure we shall see you and Sarah again soon."

"Yes, it's time for me to go as well," said Sarah. "Doris, may I use your phone to call a cab?"

"Of course you can, my dear."

After Sarah arranged for a pick-up, Everard offered to wait with her outside.

"That's very kind of you," she said. "I'd feel much safer, if you don't mind."

The chill night air was refreshing. The radiant half-moon and its entourage of glimmering stars was the only source of light in their dark corner of the world. Sarah turned to face Everard, her eyes reflecting the dazzling starlight from the luminous night sky. It took Everard's breath away. The moon's rays on his striking features captivated her. An awkward moment of silence transpired, each transfixed by the other's presence, each too shy to say what they already knew.

"How will you get home?" she finally inquired.

"I actually don't live far from here, and it's a lovely evening for a walk."

"Do be careful," she said.

After another nervous pause, their eyes fixated on each other, Everard said, "Sarah, I'd love to take you to dinner tomorrow if you're free." He knew it was a presumptuous request, not knowing if she was romantically involved with anyone. He decided it was worth the risk.

"Oh, that would be great!" She thought, *That came across a little too excited. I need to get a grip here.* "I do have to work tomorrow, but I have enough time to run home and change. Would six o'clock be okay?"

"That's perfect! I know of a quaint café that offers delicious vegetarian meals. You won't be disappointed. I'll pick you up at six then."

The taxi arrived, much too quickly, to Sarah's chagrin. Everard opened the door for her, and she stepped into the back seat feeling too elated and nervous to say or do anything beyond thank you.

"Erm ... Sarah? May I have your address and phone number please?"

They both laughed, Sarah feeling quite embarrassed. "Oh, sorry! Of course."

He took the slip of paper, shut her car door, and watched the car whisk her away until its taillights vanished into the darkness.

Chapter 5

Sarah returned to work the following day in high spirits, and it did not go unnoticed. By the end of the shift, all of her colleagues had heard about her new love interest and the juicy titbits about his good looks and genteel personality. Some gave her the green-eyed monster stare, which surprised her, but she determined that it's at times like these when one knows who their real friends are. *Never mind*, she thought. *It's not worth thinking about.*

During her rounds, she assessed Richie's wounds and changed his dressings. "This is coming along nicely. You may not need dressing changes after today, but I'll check with the doctor."

"Sounds great. As much as I like you, I'm dying to get out of here! By the way, you look especially happy today. Anything special going on?"

"Well, I shouldn't be sharing this with you, but since you asked, I met your friend, Everard, and we're going on a date tonight. He seems really nice."

"Oh, no! And here I thought I had a chance," he said with a sly giggle. "Just kidding. Everard is as genuine and caring as he looks though no one should mistake his do-good character for weakness. Inside, he's a lionhearted fighter and can roar like one too. You're a lucky lady, Miss."

***

Everard wasn't quite prepared for the stunner that greeted him when she opened her door. "Wow, you look amazing!" He bashfully handed her the modest bouquet of pink roses and planted a kiss on her cheek.

"Thank you, Everard. They're gorgeous!" she gushed as she took a whiff of the aromatic flowers. "Give me a minute while I put them in a vase."

"You have a very nice place, Sarah," he said as he eyed her sitting room. Her lounge and open kitchenette were quite small but smartly decorated in a two-tone palette of beige and sage green with compact seating that made the place feel inviting and cosy.

"Why, thank you, Everard. I know it's small and simple, but I managed to make it my own with what I could afford. Right ... ready." She called out into the next room, presumably her bedroom, "Good night, Eugene. Be back soon!"

Everard turned to her wide-eyed. "You have a roommate?"

"Oh, no," she giggled. "That's my cat, Eugene. He's tucked himself in for the night on my bed."

Everard breathed in an audible sigh of relief.

They hailed a cab which took them to a restaurant off the beaten track in Soho. Everard had made reservations, and they were promptly escorted to a table for two in a quiet corner opposite the entrance. The ambience was casual and unpretentious, with low overhead lighting and votive candles on each table flanked by bud vases with yellow daisies. Soft jazz played in the background. The waiter approached for drink requests, and after consulting with Sarah, he ordered a bottle of red wine.

"This is a lovely place, Everard. Thank you. It's perfect."

"I'm glad you like it. So tell me about your day. Hope it wasn't too hectic."

She went on to tell him and gave him an update on Richie's progress.

"That's great to hear," Everard said. "I plan to visit him in the next day or two." *She looks absolutely ravishing*, Everard thought while lost in her eyes, gazing, wondering. Finally, he found his voice. "So, Sarah, tell me more about yourself."

"Ooh, that's quite an open-ended question. Where do I start, from birth?"

"Start wherever you like. I'm all ears."

"Well, I don't remember anything about my early childhood until I started primary school in Hounslow. I was raised by a lovely middle-aged couple who eventually told me that I had been adopted from a foster home. They didn't tell me much about my biological family except that I had been abandoned and social services was called. I don't even know if I had siblings, but my adoptive parents had two girls of their own, and I just assumed that they were my sisters until my early teens when they revealed the truth.

"They were wonderful, caring parents, and when I learned I wasn't theirs biologically, it didn't matter. They provided us with such a full, nurturing life that, honestly, it has never occurred to me to find my biological family. What would be the point?"

The waiter brought the requested bottle of wine and served each a glass before taking their orders. Everard raised his glass, "To friendship," to which Sarah toasted in kind, and they each took a sip.

"What about you, Everard?"

"My story is eerily similar. My younger sister and I were left alone while my parents went out for the evening. I believe we were about four and two years old. It wasn't the first time, so we weren't afraid. We sat on the floor to watch the telly, all bundled up in our cosy blankies. What happened next was terrifying. A window shattered, and I saw two men attempting to get in. I grabbed my sister, and we ran out the back door and to a neighbour's house, who called the police.

"By the time my parents returned, social services was there, and eventually we were sent to separate foster homes. I never saw my sister again. A few months later, I was sent to a group home, from which I ran away at fifteen, and I've been on my own ever since."

Sarah reached for Everard's hand. "Oh, my! That is so sad!"

She wanted to know more, but just then, dinner arrived and they both dug in. Sarah sensed that Everard was uncomfortable about discussing his childhood further when he changed the subject and delved into his activism. She listened attentively as he recounted in a near whisper what he and Doris were involved in and their plans to change and eliminate the rampant government corruption in greater London.

"My goodness! I'm aware of what's been going on though the newspapers seem to tell part of the story from their own political perspectives. But I had no idea who the players were that are trying to rectify the problems. Everard, I'd like to be involved and help in any way I can though my work does take a lot of my time."

"That's great, Sarah! We'd love to have you onboard. Let's meet at Doris's flat and discuss what needs to be done. I'll give Doris a call to see when she's available and work the meeting around your schedule."

"Sounds like a plan," said Sarah excitedly.

They chatted on long after the food was cleared and the wine bottle emptied. Feeling tipsy and giggly, they walked arm-in-arm towards the main thoroughfare to hail a cab. The cool night air made Sarah shiver, and Everard put his arm around her shoulders. He dropped her off at her flat and asked the driver to give him a minute.

The embrace was silent, lingering, the scent of her hair intoxicating. She felt warm and secure in his arms. The kiss was soft, sensual, arousing. It was magical.

"Thank you again for a lovely evening, Everard."

"I'll give you a call in a day or two," he said. He waited in the car until he saw her enter her building safely and deeply breathed in the lingering sweetness of her scent on his hands.

Chapter 6

"Stone me, Snobby! Who the hell done this? Look at that fuckin' skip! Bloody thing's stuck in the damn doorway!"

Snobby Pyles was not amused. Pikey Pyles sniffed the air and considered emigrating to Esher.

"Two things, Pikey. First, moderate your language. It is offensive to my sensibilities. Secondly, whose fuckin' skip is that?" Snobby was feeling a sense of insecurity. He had been a bully all his life and suddenly somebody had challenged him.

"It's bloody well ours! I mean, you know, your lot, or should I say it's that Romanian git you gave a job to. It's got his bleedin' moniker on it. Look at that! It says *Raab's Rubbish*, and they've painted over the bit which says *House Clearance*. They're takin' the piss, ain't they!"

"Where's the truck? Get the driver and string 'im up and give 'im a drink of sulphuric. Nobody does this to Snobby Pyles, and I ain't standing for this shit!" Snobby was sweating and started to scratch around his collar.

"The bastards, bastards, bastards!" Pikey hacked loudly and spat a wad of thick phlegm on the sidewalk.

The vehicle that brought the skip had been found at the end of the road. The person now occupying the driver's seat was one of Snobby's own men and one of his most loyal fans. But there he was, fast asleep in a deep opioid coma unaware that a nightmare was about to replace his fairyland dreams.

Pikey yanked his victim sharply out of the cab. Despite the crunch as he hit the ground, it was the first kick in his ear that was the man's moment of awakening. The second removed an eye, and the third broke his windpipe. The acid dissolved his face. The process of his untimely demise was over in seconds. Snobby had followed his brother at a leisurely pace and was a little surprised at his brother's alacrity in disposing of the man's life.

"Too bloody quick, Pikey! What were you thinking? Now we won't know who set 'im up! What are we goin' to do with all that rot? My god, what 'ave I done to deserve this? It ain't you, is it, Pikey? You ain't done all this, 'ave yer? Wantin' to take over, do yer? Trying to make me look stupid? Is that it, Pikey? You fuckin' bastard!"

As Snobby was hollering, Pikey had been gradually collapsing to his knees. From a small red hole in his forehead, a gentle trickle of blood oozed its way down the side of his nose. Pikey was no longer responsive to his brother's raving. In disbelief that his brother was silent for once, Snobby turned around and was surprised to see the inert figure lying at his feet.

"Come on, Pikey, get up, will yer!" The sudden realization stunned him. "Stone me! The bugger's dead!"

Snobby did not like dead people, and his brother was no exception. He had always felt that Pikey was his superior, and Pikey had always known it. His death was a benefit to Snobby in that respect. He would no longer feel his lowness in the eyes of his illustrious brother, though within himself, Snobby had nothing to boast about.

He was not tall, only five feet seven on slightly raised shoe heels, had false teeth since he was ten years old, and stunk of cheap aftershave—actually a costly commodity which just smelled cheap on him. His bad humour had permanently fostered a build-up of white froth at the corners of his lips which sometimes left little white flecks down his jacket lapels, shirt and tie. Unlike dandruff, they were harder to brush away. To avoid this unsightly phenomenon, he had taken to wearing small polka-dotted shirts and a white jacket and tie. All one could say in his favour was that despite his floppy lips, shaved head, pot belly, and aggressive attitude, he actually looked quite tough.

Lou Pole, an uncomplicated, long-legged, Caribbean man was jogging past on the other side of the road, taking his afternoon run in training for the London Marathon. In the moments that followed, he wished he hadn't been there at all, having had a distinct desire to run very fast, far away from what he knew was not going to be a congenial adventure.

"Here, you! Whatever your bleedin' name is! Get over here and start clearing this lot up! There's a shovel in the back of that van and a large black bag. Shove my brother in it and take him down to the tip. I ain't wasting good money on a bleedin' funeral! Now, get bloody moving, you shit!"

Snobby thought he had everything under control, but Lou didn't know who Snobby Pyles actually was, having only recently arrived on that particular piece of turf, owned and run by the aggressive spiv who now stood red-faced across the road from him. It was a moment of truth for Snobby. Nobody had dared to stand up against him, but here was a man who just stood there looking at him with a dumbfounded expression.

"What's the matter with you? Are you the founder of the deaf-and-dumb society, or are you just plain bloody stupid? Now, do it or else!"

Besides other things, Lou was actually deaf and had no idea what Snobby was telling him to do. He was too intent on watching Snobby's index finger as it jabbed incessantly across the road towards the bewildered man. Lou realised at last that he was being threatened, and believing that an attack on an aggressor was always preferable to getting a beating, he ran across the road and punched Snobby fair and square on the end of his nose.

It hurt Snobby, both physically and mentally, but within a second, Snobby was lashing out at Lou with a very large flick knife. Lou fled with the enraged Snobby close on his heels. He took the first right turn into the dead end of Gove Alley and raced through the open gateway of a derelict warehouse hoping to find somewhere to hide. Instead, he was confronted with a vast building site with disused machinery rusting on a vista of rubble. Undaunted, he paced onwards across the divide towards what he could see and hoped was civilisation and safety.

Snobby continued in hot pursuit for another fifteen minutes when Lou turned the corner of Truss Street and out of the East End. It was here that a foot conveniently protruded from a doorway, catching Snobby's ankle as he chased his prey, bringing the panting animal to the floor, his flick knife clattering onto the pavement in front of him. Before long, he had attracted the attention of the passing crowd.

A kindly woman in her late sixties with a small brown dog was the first and only person to approach the fallen gangster. "Are you alright, young man? Were you chasing that poor chap with the big knife that you've just dropped on the pavement? I'd better put it out of harm's way, hadn't I?" Turning, she trod on Snobby's right hand, giving her heel a slight twist at the same time.

"Oh dear, I'm so sorry! I didn't mean to be so clumsy!" She picked up the weapon and turning back to Snobby, she suggested, "This is a pretty thing, isn't it now? I could use this to get rid of a few morons who fancy themselves as gangsters. Do you think that would be a good idea, Mr. Snobby Pyles?"

Snobby couldn't believe it. Not only did she know his name, but people were actually beginning to laugh at him as more and more bystanders gathered to watch his degradation. What he didn't realise was how far he had chased Lou. He was now outside his own domain and had somehow ended up in the land of milk and honey.

"I think he has strayed a little too far, don't you think, Molly?" she asked her dog.

"I do believe he has," replied the dog, looking up with a quizzical smile.

"So what do you think we should do with him, Molly?"

"He doesn't smell very nice! I think he needs a little perfume to remind him that he doesn't belong here!" With that, Molly backed up towards the creature who had by this time adopted a foetal position. Raising her tail and in a semi-squatting attitude, she ejected a fast but accurate jet of urine, drenching Snobby's trousers at crotch level.

"Look at that, Molly. I think he's wet himself!" said Doris. The crowd laughed on cue as Snobby Pyles raised himself from the ground, choking in an impotent rage. The crowd gathered around him, pointing and jeering at him with calls of "Wet yourself, have you, Snobby?" and "Better get home to mummy. Go on, off you go!" but every time he tried to push his way out, he was met with resistance and was quickly pushed back into the centre of the mêlée.

After a short period of jostling and giggling, it was as if somebody had blown a whistle or clapped their hands because the assembled audience turned away en masse. Each person took up their previous activity as if nothing had happened, leaving Snobby alone except for one woman and her dog.

"What's that on your chest, Snobby?"

Snobby looked down at the little red dot on the lapel of his jacket. He tried to brush it away, but as if in fun with a mind of its own, it slipped down his front, down to his genital area, where it rotated in a tight circle. Snobby wanted to scream.

"I'll get you and your lot! I'll have you and your bloody dog on my plate before the week's out. You, you bloody witch, you see if I don't!"

Doris quietly walked away, talking softly to Molly.

"Well that was funny, wasn't it, Molly!"

"Yes," Molly replied, "I laughed so much I nearly wet myself."

Snobby, having endured his round of abuse, turned to leave but was confronted by a man, impressive in stature, around six feet six, carrying a large pie which he duly rubbed with gusto into the face of the raving gangster.

It was the last straw. Snobby Pyles, a man feared throughout East London from Elephant to Tottenham, wept, totally demoralised. He looked down at himself, custard and pastry smeared down his jacket and shirt, his hair matted and his trousers soaked with urine. He thought of his brother still lying dead a few miles away. *Where's my damn gang? How the hell did this happen to me? ME, Snobby Pyle!*

It was no better when he arrived back, still on foot, to his own territory. Everyone who saw him covered their mouths in case they were seen to be amused by the spectacle of the crestfallen thug.

He returned to the site of his brother's demise and looked forlornly down at the corpse, gently bending forward to brush away the bluebottles that were already accessing the nostrils and mouth of the dead body. As he looked up, his gaze met with the worried faces of his most loyal adherents, each looking down at him with an unlikely pity, for they were, in their own skins, normally void of pity.

"For Christ's sakes, you lot! What are you staring at! It's a blip, that's all, a bloody great blip. Now get this lot sorted and get my brother down to Lucan and Kydde. Tell them that I'm doin' them a favour and that I ain't paying for this one 'cause they owe me. Remind them I've sent a lot of business their way. Tell them that they better do it well or they'll pay big time! By the way, that stupid fat git lying by the skip lorry? Chuck 'im into the skip along with that load of crap where he belongs."

There was a general sigh of relief from his minions, most of whom relied entirely on Snobby for their income. The idea that he might be demoralised (if that's the word for it) by the day's events could mean that they would have to join the queue at the Job Centre, being no longer on the payroll of the mobster.

Snobby's requests were met with an eager willingness to please with calls of "Yes, boss!" Anyone watching would think that if he had told them to gather moondust and gave them a balloon in which to carry it away, they would have been equally pleased to do so. Such was their dependence on Snobby Pyles.

***

Several days passed without much happening in Snobby's world. He no longer smelled of dog wee, the stench around his club slightly dissipated, the steps washed and disinfected. A stiff south-westerly wind helped with the ventilation. He felt a little relieved that Pikey was out of the picture, that he wouldn't have to share the proceeds of the protection, prostitution, and drug rackets of which he was now the sole controller.

But complacency has its price. He had barely noticed that some of the regular faces were missing. It was only when Constable Robbie Higgitt made him a personal visit that Snobby thought he'd better do a head count.

"Snobby, don't you know that Billy, Gobby, Satchel and Smith are down at the mortuary awaiting your identification? Apparently, they all put you down as next of kin, but Satchel thought it should be spelled k-i-n-e, which is German for cattle or something, I think. You'll need to pick up their personal effects as well, but I've got their guns and razors in a bag in the boot of the car. If you like, I'll give Lucan and Kydde a ring after you've seen them."

"Nah, leave that to me. Where did you find my boys anyway, and how did they get done in?"

"Well, that's difficult to say. They were all run over by a bus. Not all at once, though. It seems that they were crawling out of manholes on Oxford Street—different holes, different buses—but all knocked clean dead. It's quite bizarre. Never seen anything like it! But Snobby, what were they doing on Oxford

Street? That's not your turf, is it, or are you looking to make alliances?"

"That ain't none of your business, even if I was. But as for them, all I can think is that they must have lost their way down in the sewers and must have been looking for each other."

"That seems reasonable, Snobby. I'll put that forward as an obvious conclusion, and it should make it easier to close the case. By the way, it was lucky that the guys in the car who found your blokes are sympathetic and passed their weaponry over to our station without reporting it to their own. Try to remember them with a little something. It will be worthwhile for you and me and make things easier on another occasion should it arise."

After the policeman left, Snobby thought that it was necessary to go to the mortuary as quickly as possible. Something seriously bothered him and that was the claim that he was next of kin. It didn't make sense. All of them had partners of one kind or another and a couple even had children. So why had they made him next of kin?

He was soon to find out. As each corpse was revealed, Snobby noticed the tell-tale signs that each of them had been bound, wrists and ankles. He concluded that all of them had been in no position to resist the oncoming buses, probably held in position up to the moment of their deaths. Snobby suddenly realised that he had become seriously vulnerable ... but to whom? Who was the woman with the dog, the man with the custard pie, the deaf man? What was going on?

Snobby's first thought was that he had been set up, in which case he was the dupe of a very clever plot. How did he fall into it so easily? He looked back at the events, and he could not understand how it all came together with him in the middle completely degraded.

The bastards! They can't do this to me! I'm Snobby Pyles!

But they had, and he knew it. As he left the mortuary, other questions came to him: *If my boys were captive and then run over by buses, how was it that they were still armed?* That certainly didn't make any sense. Was Constable Higgitt part of the plot? Why were his boys in the West End? They should have been working the East End. Who were these two coppers who handed the weapons over? He sat on a park bench to mull these questions over.

Pigeons are not noted for their humour nor for compassion. True to form, one of their flock, for whatever reason, emptied its bowels with such accuracy and aplomb that Snobby Pyles felt the warmth of a moderately large parcel of excrement upon the brim of his trilby, pushing it down over his brow and dripping the more liquid part of it down over his nose and across his lips. Snobby Pyles had but one response. "Aarrgh!"

The day, he felt, had been far too long.

Chapter 7

After their first enchanting date, Sarah and Everard had phoned or met almost every evening, and the more they learned about each other, the more connected they felt. On this rainy evening, they had been invited to Doris's place for dinner and drinks with the Blakes. Sarah brought her delicious bread-and-butter pudding for dessert, and on their way there, Everard picked up flowers for Doris and treats for Molly.

Everard sat in a cosy armchair across from Sarah, and it was evident that he could not keep his eyes off her as she sat demurely with her slender legs crossed.

Then he saw it.

He shut his eyes tightly and reopened them, hoping it was just an illusion. But it wasn't. He could almost sense the blood draining from his face, his thoughts reeling, his body frozen. *This can't be!*

Gathering himself together, Everard excused himself and took Doris into the kitchen.

"What's wrong? You look like you just saw a ghost. What's happening?" Doris asked.

"Doris, I'm having a hard time coming to terms with this. I just noticed that Sarah has a distinctive scar just below her right knee that I remember from when I was a child. Ask her how she got it because I believe it was from a piece of flying glass when our childhood home was broken into. My parents left my younger sister and I alone that night. Social services took us away and put us into care separately. I never saw my sister nor my parents again.

"I was four then and she was two when they took us, but I remember that scar on her leg after it healed. Find out what she remembers, please. Doris, I think Sarah is my sister. I need to know. What am I going to do? Doris, I'm in love with her!"

"Oh, dear! So that's the problem, and what a problem! Calm down and let's find out the facts first. That we are all here must be a sign that this is the right time for you two to reconnect the right way. So go back in there and ask Sarah to give me a hand and have a chat with Richie's parents. They will need reassurance over the next few weeks. Go on, off you go! Oh, by the way, Everard. How old are you?"

"Twenty-six. She should be twenty-four if she is my sister."

Everard returned to the lounge, offered everyone another glass of wine, and nonchalantly suggested to Sarah that Doris was in need of assistance. Sarah joined Doris while Everard tried to keep Richie's parents and himself on an even keel.

A few minutes later, Doris entered the lounge holding a dishcloth. "Everard, excuse me for a minute, but what was you sister's second name?"

"Louise. Why?"

"Sarah, can you come in here for a minute, please?" she called out. "Come and meet your brother."

***

Sarah was as stunned as Everard was confused. They stood there in the dining room of Doris's apartment staring at each other. Everard eventually broke the impasse.

"It's the scar under your knee, Sarah. That's how I knew, and I remember how it happened. I was there with you when the window was broken and those men came in. When they smashed the window, a piece of glass flew across the room and cut your leg. There was a lot of blood and you cried, and I didn't know what to do.

"When our parents returned, the police were there, and it was chaos with everybody shouting at each other. It was a couple of weeks later that some people came and took us away, and we never saw Mum and Dad ever again. I thought I'd lost you forever as well. But we must have stayed at home for a little while because your leg had nearly healed by the time we were separated. I suppose it took some time for them to find us foster homes. Sarah, I don't know what else to say right now. I'm completely lost."

Sarah was still trying to come to grips with this devastating revelation. "Well, Everard, it certainly explains a lot. I can't remember anything about it because I was so young. But I often felt that there was something missing, a kind of longing, and I could never think of what it was until my adoptive parents explained it."

Everard reached out and held Sarah while she silently wept in his arms. Doris, Lyn, and Alan slipped into the kitchen to give them the privacy they needed.

Everard, breaking the embrace, vented, "I wanted you to be my girl, but now I've got you as a sister to look after. It's not bloody fair!" Everard caught himself. "Oh, I'm sorry. I didn't mean it that way." Having said too much, he pulled Sarah to him, and they embraced once again.

Sarah whispered in his ear, "Everard, I'm in love with you, and I'm not really sure how to manage this either. Do we resolve to overcome our love for each other, avoid temptation, and behave like brother and sister from now on? Frankly, I don't think that's possible."

Everard looked at Sarah with a slightly bedevilled stare. "I don't think so either. We met as strangers, and our feelings for each other have gone too far and are too strong to undo or ignore them. I see you as my love, my soulmate. There is no going back. Even after knowing, I want you the way a man wants a woman."

He ran his fingers through her hair and whispered, "God, Sarah, you are so, so ... " She placed her fingers across his lips before he could finish the sentence. They continued to embrace, Everard with his hands at the top of her buttocks, his fingers pressing lightly into her skin. She responded with an even closer embrace, oblivious of their surroundings.

Richie's mum's phone rang, and they heard Lyn confirm that she was Richie's mother.

The voice on the other end explained, "I'm calling regarding a young lad in the burn unit, Richie Blake. There is a couple here wanting to take him home. They say that they are his parents, but I have your number as belonging to his mother. What would you like me to tell them, or do you want the police called?"

"My god, stop them! They're impostors. Call the police and get your security to hold them. We'll get to the hospital as quickly as possible. Don't let them take Richie!"

Doris was already on her own phone and demanded, "Car here at once to the Royal Free, insurance required, attack imminent!" Having finished her call before Lyn had, she tried to reassure the worried parents that everything would be fine and that Richie would be safe. "We'll be there in a jiffy. There's a car on its way to take us."

Doris had barely gotten her words out when her phone rang three times then stopped.

"Quick—Lyn, Alan—the car is here. Everard, Sarah, please stay here and look after the dinner. We'll be back soon, hopefully with Richie." With that, they were gone.

Everard went to the window, but looking down, he could see nothing. "Dammit! It's almost like a film. People vanish into thin air and then pop up again without any explanation. You know, Sarah, all this started outside a post office when I tried to help some old people. I started it, but for some reason, I can't figure out who is running things now. Doris deals with it all and keeps me completely out of it. It never fails to surprise me what she gets up to."

"Who would think that Doris walking Molly down the road would ever be the mistress of all she surveys. But Everard, aren't you pleased that you found her, and through her, me?"

Sarah smiled at Everard with a somewhat sultry invitation to her lips, totally unnerving Everard.

"God, Sarah! Don't do that. We're meant to be looking after the meal and it'll burn if we … " But it was too late as Sarah closed in on him.

***

Doris's car and Richie's parents' car were approaching the hospital when another vehicle shot past them in the opposite direction. Immediately, the insurance car that Doris had requested turned sharply behind the speeding vehicle and made chase. As far as they were concerned, the quarry was in foreign territory and had little chance of escape. Every road that the runaway car approached was blocked by the new security.

The occupants of the car were finally captured in a cul-de-sac, giving themselves up without a fight. Richie was with them and fortunately unharmed. Under tight questioning, the husband-and-wife would-be kidnappers explained how they had become embroiled in the Richie affair.

"It's that Snobby Pyles," the husband explained. "Nobody can refuse him. Look at me! I've only got one arm, and the bastard said he'd cut the other one off if we didn't do what he said. Then he picks on Jenny and tells her that if she's got anything to say to anybody, he would send her off to the dog food factory packed up in a suitcase. What could we do? The police are working for him as well, and he soon finds out if anybody says anything against him.

"So what are you going to do to us? We really didn't want to do any of this, but we were so frightened, and I didn't want Jenny to have to wipe my bum for me if I had no arms."

By that time, Doris and Richie's parents had arrived, and Richie was at last reunited with his own family. Jenny and Sid,

Jenny's husband, apologised for what they had tried to do, and though the trauma of nearly losing their son had given them a great fright, Lyn and Alan were keen to accept the situation as it was.

The group climbed back into the two remaining vehicles — Jenny, Lyn, Doris and Richie in one and Alan and Sid in the other — and all headed back to Doris's apartment.

***

Everard and Sarah, having solidly occupied their time together, were still looking at each other in a kind of loving confusion when the doorbell rang. Suddenly, the room was filled with people.

"Is there enough food for another couple, or shall we phone out for something?" Doris was trying to be gentle, but Everard took the hint, and he and Sarah quickly departed to stock up the kitchen larder.

As the two descended the stairs, they both knew that the revelation of their kinship had little effect on their desire to love each other. The days to come would be full of disappointment if they were to adhere to the rules when all they really wanted was to be close. They held hands tightly as they disappeared into the darkness past the corner of the street. Clearly, maintaining control would be a losing emotional battle.

Each of them had had partners or lovers in the past, and those relationships at times had seemed complete. With the others, love apparently had shown itself to be fairly noncommittal, yet what they were now experiencing was nothing like that. It had been almost instant, the catalyst being that both were in one way or another looking out for young Richie.

Beyond that came an irresistible physical attraction in both shape and content. For Sarah, it was Everard's easy-going, loving nature and sensitivity. Everard adored everything about Sarah.

He couldn't help but notice her walk, the way her hips swayed with a smooth serpentine glide. Her expressions of concern, happiness, determination, concentration, and her radiant smile were such that Everard could not ignore them. There was one other thing that held them together and that was blood, the same familial blood that coursed through their veins, unifying them with an iron grip, but the collision of their forbidden passions was in danger of being all-consuming. Neither had known such feelings existed let alone experienced them. But their love was to become too deep to ignore or cast aside.

Chapter 8

When Sid and Jenny failed to return, Snobby quickly realised that his attempt to take Richie had failed. He considered calling his minions in the police force, but after the visit from Constable Higgitt the previous week, he felt that something was closing in on him, and he was beginning to miss his brother, Pikey. He had always been good at doing this sort of stuff. He always knew how to get to the truth of the matter when it was necessary and sometimes even when it wasn't. Most of his operatives were now trying to keep a low profile, and he had noticed it. He realised that to get back in control, he needed to gather them together for what might be interpreted as a pep talk.

Sunday would be a good day, he thought. Sunday afternoon after lunch and after they all returned from church. He smiled to himself being quite amused by his own humour, something for which he was not noted. And so it was that the troops arrived at four o'clock to be encouraged or reviled, to take up the sword and strike the aggressors down. Trouble was, nobody knew who the aggressors were.

Though it all seemed straightforward, nothing could be done until Rodney Crudhill suggested, "What if we contact the West End Boys, you know, Shagman's gang. They might know something."

It was a sensible suggestion, but it was met with a dangerous disdain that left Rodney Crudhill fruitlessly trying to stem the blood that flowed copiously from the slit in his throat.

Snobby carefully wiped the blood from the blade of his razor, and addressing his followers, he said, "I think it might be a good idea to contact the West End Gang and have a word with Shagman. He might know something. If not, it might have been them that left our dear friends dead and now lying cold in the bloody mortuary.

"In the meantime, Charlie and Bert, take a look at Rodney. If he's not finished dying, give him a bit of help, then get hold of Lucan and Kydde and tell them they still owe me big time despite having dealt with my brother, my dearly missed and beloved brother, Pikey. They'll know what to do. Tell them I want the acid bath. Saves on the box and handles and the fuckin' rest."

He turned and left his helpers to get on with his instructions. Nobody dared say a word.

Charlie and Bert tended to Rodney and saw that he was still not dead. Quickly they covered his face lest the others see him breathe and carried the supposed corpse out of the room. They rushed him off to the A&E in foreign terrain, the Royal Free. They knew that leaving him in any local care would be a death sentence for Rodney and themselves, so they did the only sensible thing and ran. Besides that, Rodney was family in the real sense rather than the metaphorical sense, being a first cousin to the fleeing duo.

It saved Rodney's life, for what it was worth, but gave Sarah a chance to become more involved in the great change that was affecting more and more of North London. Sarah was on duty the evening that Rodney was brought in, and following the new protocols, she informed the local agent of the secret council, that being Doris, who was charged with investigating any suspicious wounding. Being unaware of the surveillance, Charlie and Bert explained to Sarah that Rodney had cut himself shaving, but having made the call, it was not long before Mrs. Doris Wells appeared claiming to be visiting a patient who had unexpectedly discharged herself.

Hello, what ever happened to him?" she asked Charlie. "He doesn't look very well, does he now?"

Charlie was not shy about blabbering, and offering Doris a chair, he stated, "We weren't there at the time, but we think 'e cut his throat while he was shaving … probably sneezed or something. It'll take a day or two to heal, that's for sure."

"Well, well, well! Fancy that, now! One of Snobby Pyles's boys cutting his throat while shaving. That's almost laughable!" As she spoke, she never once looked at the brothers, only at Snobby's victim, Rodney.

"Snobby who? Never heard of 'im! Who is 'e anyway?" Charlie's denial was far from convincing.

Doris was not playing any more. "Stop the BS! You're making a fool of yourself. I know you're Snobby Pyles's lads, but what I want to know is why you are here. Why isn't he in your own hospital, A&E? I suspect the answer to that is that you have all done a runner. So I take it that this chap in the bed has had his throat cut by either of you or your boss. Now, you are in dangerous territory, and I believe that you have no idea how you're going to survive in this very hostile environment. The truth is that you will only survive if you're honest.

"Now, I'm taking a chance, and I'm going to hand you and what's-his-name here to the ruling council. They'll know if you're lying, so be very, very careful and stick to the truth. Got it?"

It was what the two really wanted. It was a chance to remove the chains by which Snobby Pyles had held them in check. Charlie and Bert thanked Doris for being straight with them and appeared quite contrite that they had tried to deceive her.

Charlie offered more, "We can't go back. He'll have us fed to the dogs, piece by piece. Look, Rodney here is our cousin, and all he did was make a suggestion which Snobby then claimed was his idea, and then he cut Rodney's throat. The man's a monster. He told us to take him to Lucan & Kydde, the undertakers, after we finished him off and to tell them to chuck him in an acid bath to save on the funeral cost.

"We couldn't do it. Rodney is family, and he's not a violent bloke. Okay, we've done some very, very bad things doing what Snobby and his brother Pikey told us to do. Some things were so bad that we're ashamed to even talk about them, but Snobby made us, sort of boasting about how cruel we were in doing his bidding. It's all a really bad business, and we don't ever want to get caught up in that sort of thing again. We never really wanted to, but he caught us when we were too young to know what he really had in mind."

Bert broke his silence with an almost pleading expression. "Honest, Missus, it's true! He got us doing his bidding when we were about twelve years old. He had us collecting the money from his girls and telling the other youngsters, boys that is, where they had to go to service a bunch of rich blokes, some of them in power, if you see what I mean. It's all been a bloody nightmare. It's only now that we have run for it that we can look back and regret all what we got ourselves into."

Charlie never used a swear word in all that he had said, nor had Bert, and from that alone, Doris could see that the two, maybe even Rodney if he survived, could be of significant use in the rescue of the communities that existed on the edge of penury whilst living under the shadow of Snobby Pyles.

A sudden commotion in the corridor outside the room, a shuffling of resisting feet, and a stifled objection broke off their conversation. Sarah was unceremoniously and violently thrust into the room, shoved forward from behind by none other than … Snobby Pyles.

"I thought I'd find you lot in here and with, don't tell me, the old besom who gave me a rollicking a little while ago. So while I've got my knife ready to gut this young lady if you don't do as I say, then it will be goodbye to the lot of you.

"Bert, I told you and Charlie to get Rodney down to Lucan and Kydde. Now pick up that pillow there and hold it over his face 'till he don't move no more. And Charlie, this old gossip who you've been telling your life story to, I want you to strangle her in front of me, just so I know that you've done it right. And when you're done, I want you two to hold this young woman while I do her, and when I'm done, I want you two to do the same as me. Then you will kill her. I'll have to think about that properly, though ... something memorable and preferably very, very painful. You got me? Now do it!"

During his rant, Snobby had lost sight of his environment and was totally unaware of the presence of Everard, who was standing very quietly behind him. Not wanting to make any sudden movement that may jeopardise Sarah or anyone else, Everard remained totally silent while he figured out what to do. There weren't too many options, but one thing struck him as being a possibility ... people do not like being stung by insects.

Taking the safety pin from the top of his fly—his zip was not reliable—he suddenly made a sharp buzzing noise just behind Snobby's ear, and at the same time, jabbed the man's neck with the point of the pin. The reaction was just as he'd hoped. Snobby spun round only to feel Everard's brow smash hard into his nose. Dazed, Snobby fell backwards into Charlie, who decided that the fall might crack open his ex-boss's head. Thus, he let him continue in the downward trajectory with a simple step backwards. It didn't quite work, but it did give Snobby a good deal of pain from both his nose and the back of his head. Game over.

Snobby was bound and gagged, covered with a sheet, and transported on a trolley out to a waiting private ambulance which took him swiftly back to the East End.

***

Seeing a body lying in the gutter covered in bandages and gagged is always likely to gain curiosity from anybody who, by chance, might be passing by. In the course of ten minutes, Snobby Pyles was in the centre of a crowd of bystanders, none of whom dared to touch him, not knowing who he was nor what kind of malady had left him in such a state.

At last, one of the kids from the playground noted the eyes despite the tears and declared, "Ere! That's bloody Snobby Pyles! Look at 'em eyes. Gor! Whatever 'appened to 'im!"

The crowd slipped away one by one, not wanting to be seen laughing. Only one person took pity on him and covered him with a couple of black refuse bags. Snobby laid there for another three days until the binmen picked him up and chucked him into their truck to join the rest of the East End detritus. It was at this point that the strapping finally broke, and ripping off the gag, Snobby was able to scream, "Oi! Don't fuckin' crush me! I'm a bleedin' 'uman being!"

The statement was risible, but for the sake of humanity, the binmen stopped the machine just as it had started to compress Snobby along with masses and messes, from the cat litter to pig swill, from compost to bathroom waste. It was amazing that the men were able to differentiate between the scrap and the human scourge and were able to see him. They left him in the gutter but now standing, with an audience unable to hold its mirth any longer. Snobby Pyles was finished, filmed with a large rotten tomato, reminiscent of a broken pork-pie hat, sliding down his forehead. The picture was quickly released in the papers for the whole world to see.

***

Earlier, as Snobby was being carried away from the hospital, Sarah was almost in a state of amnesia for, bearing in mind that Everard was her newfound brother, she pulled her saviour to her and kissed him as she had never kissed anyone before. Everard felt his passion rise, and hugging her to himself, the two were locked in an embrace that seemed to have no end. Doris coughed and ushered the two brothers, Charlie and Bert, out of the room to let the lovers find themselves in their deep but otherwise illicit affair.

Outside, Doris was joined by a small group of rather shadowy figures who unnerved the brothers by their sombre anonymity. Doris was firm, if not a little threatening in her approach.

"Right! Your boss is finished, and it seems to me that you have arrived in this part of town in a call to find some kind of asylum. With your previous record of unbridled violence against the innocent people in the East End, why should we grant you safe conduct when we basically will have nothing to be gained from it? Granted it took some courage for you to come here, but I think you really had no choice. So, what now? What have you got to say for yourselves?"

After a stuttering start, Bert blurted out, "We can help you in what you're doing. We know a lot of people who thought Snobby was good for them because they lived off what he was taking and were protected by him and his brother, Pikey. You know Pikey was shot dead, don't you?"

Doris replied curtly, "Of course I do! It was necessary to take him out of the picture."

"Do you mean that you shot him?" Charlie blustered. He had trouble believing that an older female could have done such a thing. Doris said nothing but turned her head and uttered something to a member of her entourage.

"Snobby is probably still alive, so are you going back to work for him or against him? Rodney will be here for a good while yet, but at least he will be safe. Make your choice but bear in mind that whatever it is, you aren't going to have an easy time either here or out there in the East End."

Charlie looked worried and confused. "We don't know what to do. We've got nowhere to live, and we came away without any cash. Neither of us has got a bank account 'cause Snobby always paid us in cash. We can't go back, that's for sure. If Snobby sees us, he will find some way to kill us. On the other hand, if he is finished as you say, then the locals will probably kill us. Either way, we're done." Charlie sat down outside Rodney's room with his head in his hands.

Doris's tone softened a little. "Well, you obviously need to stay in our area until we have sorted the East End out, which may take some time. Let's face it, Snobby was just one of many, and until they've all been eliminated, it won't be safe for you to return. I suggest that you go to the Help Centre at Muswell Hill. They will give you some tokens for food and tell you where you can bunk down for the night. They might also give you a small amount of cash, probably a fiver each, for your fares to the Job Centre and the Social Security Office.

"Remember, things have changed. Here the people rule and not the government of the rest of this godforsaken country. Here's the taxi fare to Muswell Hill, and tomorrow, take whatever the security offers you. Proper work will sort you out and give you a regular income. Accommodation will follow if the scheme of empty property acquisition continues at the present pace. Now, off you go, and don't mess it up or you'll be fed back to the East End. Just knuckle down. It's a new start, a chance to live as human beings rather than as savage animals."

The pair called their goodbyes to Rodney through the door and were escorted to the exit where a taxi was waiting to take them to Muswell Hill.

Their lives had taken a violent turn, and they were unsure of what was likely to happen. Not for a long time had they been frightened or felt insecurity, and there seemed to be no end to that fear in sight. However, in time, they would get used to it, a time when they might understand that there was nothing more to fear than fear itself.

***

Doris looked into Rodney's room, noticed that Everard and Sarah were still in a clasp and said, "I'll see you two later at the flat. We need to talk."

Everard looked round with a smile. "I think I know what you want to discuss. Something about brotherly love?"

"Yes, that and other things. The bigger the situation, the more difficult it is to keep a grip on it all. I'm getting a bit too old to carry on much longer, so since you started it all, I think you should be a little more involved, and it might keep your mind off other things." Doris gave them a stern look and turned to go.

"We'll see you later, Doris. By the way, are Richie's parents still with you today or have they gone to look at a new place to live?"

"I think the ruling council has found some space for them and arranged for a nurse to do home visits. As far as I know, they are all safe as a family again. By the way, Everard, I want to adopt Molly. She spends more time with me now, and I have become very attached to her. Is that alright with you?"

"You'll have to ask Molly. We could share her, I suppose, couldn't we?"

"Only if you live long enough to be a sharer. That last stunt with that old bloke, Snobby's spy, was a bit close to the bone and you see what came of it. Richie in hospital, me having to sort Snobby out in the street, nothing but bad news. Just be a bit more bloody careful, for heaven's sakes! It caused a lot of trouble and left us with a whole new set of problems."

"See you later Doris. We'll talk then, shall we?"

"Yes, all four of us—you, Sarah, Molly and me. So bring a bottle or two of decent wine and some special dog food, and if you're good, I'll make a goulash. You're not on duty tonight, are you Sarah?"

"No, I've got a couple of days off before the next shift, but I'll need to check on my flat this afternoon just to make sure everything's okay. Will you come back with me, Everard?"

Doris finally made her way out of the hospital and was escorted back to her own apartment, which seemed to have gotten smaller with the constant comings and goings. *What would I have done without Snobby?* she thought. *Molly and I could have retired ages ago!*

***

Molly was eagerly waiting by the door as Doris entered her flat.

"Where have you been? I want to have a poo, and I don't know how much longer I can hold out. Quick, take my lead and fetch the doggie bag!"

"Molly, I'm a lot older than you. Just slow down for a minute while I get my walkie shoes on."

Off they went with Molly leading the way to the bush at the end of the road. The bit Doris hated most was that the deposit was warm and soft, and it always felt as if the bag was never thick enough to contain the elements within. But it did, and everything was over in a few minutes, the bag quickly disposed into one of the many special depositories that were now to be found at the end of every street.

"You know, Molly, all your poo goes to the big composter behind the barn in the park, and then it's given away to anybody with an allotment. But I must say, I'd hate to be the one to empty all the bags."

Molly smiled, "Shall I see if I can do a bit more?"

"I think it's enough for the moment, really. I need to get back to do some cooking. Come on, back we go!"

Chapter 9

Sarah and Everard returned to Sarah's flat. It was the first time that they had been truly alone together and now began to realize how problematic their relationship had become. Everard knew that if he was to take a more active role in the new society of North London, then Sarah would be in even more danger.

"Sarah, I really like your flat but it must be quite expensive to rent, or do you own it?" he enquired.

"My adoptive parents own it but have given me a free lifetime lease on it. If anything happens to them, then I will inherit it. So, it's as good as mine. There is only one proviso and that is if anyone else comes to live with me, they'll have to pay a rent of £200 per month. But that is really cheap for accommodation in this area. I mean it's got a bedroom with plenty of light, and all the rooms are quite spacious, even the bath-shower room. What's your place like?"

"Rubbish. That's the only way to describe it in comparison to this. And it costs me a small fortune every month." Everard knew what was to follow and almost dreaded it, but at the same time, he hoped she would say it.

"Would you like to move in with me, Everard? We don't have to tell anyone we're related, but even as brother and sister, it would still not be too unusual. I know it happens quite a lot and nobody says a word. Well, not out loud anyway."

Everard could not contain himself despite any misgivings. "Sarah, Sarah! Yes, yes, yes! How could I ever say no to such a proposition? The idea of being with you is so ... When can I bring my stuff over? There's not much, just my laptop, a few clothes, and a couple of dog bowls. Everything else belongs to the landlord, and he can keep it. It's all junk."

"It's settled, then!" Sarah replied, half laughing. "I'll get you a new set of keys so you can bring over whatever you want, whenever you want. Are you going to tell Doris? She's not too happy about all of this, is she?" Sarah poured out some tea, and together they sat wondering how to deal with their dilemma without shaking too much fruit from the trees.

"Look, Sarah, we are brother and sister, and it is necessary for us to look out for each other, especially under the present crisis, and the only way we can do it is to live together, isn't it!" Everard tried to look serious, but Sarah burst out laughing.

Ignoring her mirth, he continued. "That's easier for people to understand. If we stick to that, nobody can say it's wrong to be together. Even Doris will have to accept that, whether she believes it or not. And even if she doesn't, we don't owe anyone an explanation as to what happens behind closed doors."

Everard was already beginning to feel weak-kneed in anticipation of spending more time in Sarah's company, and became curious as to what the rest of the flat was like. He looked around, found the loo and the shower, tried the kitchen taps, and even looked inside the washing machine.

Having watched him for a short while, Sarah called to him, "Everard, dear, what on earth are you doing?"

"Trying to be calm and look intelligent."

"Well, you're not doing too well, are you, then?" Sarah retorted with laughter in her voice. "Everard, come here and put your arms around me."

And that is precisely what he did. Their embrace progressed naturally, unhurriedly, kindled by their inner fires and the freedom rendered by their solitude.

By half past five, they were both on their way to spend the evening with Doris and Molly.

***

Doris knew that whatever she said would have absolutely no effect on the young lovers, and they knew it too. As a result, the subject was barely touched upon, and it was the situation in the East End that carried the conversation for the evening. However, Doris did have one question, something that puzzled her.

"What was it that attracted you two to each other? I'm really curious."

"It was the old lady in the taxi. She was somewhat deranged, but Everard was so kind to her. With Richie, he really did work hard to give him a chance at a new life. He is brave and kind, and I think he is very honest and also good company. What else can I add except that I love him, and I felt that magnetism almost from our first meeting."

"And you, Everard?" Doris had a distinctively devilish look in her eyes.

"Sarah had waited for Richie all afternoon, and it said a lot about her patience and desire to do for others. In the taxi, she was so comforting and compassionate towards the confused old woman. Obviously, what first caught my eye was how beautiful she is, and instantly, I wanted to know her better. Call it love at first sight, if you like. It really doesn't matter.

"Not having been brought up together within a family, we never got to develop that sibling bond that would have enabled us to relate on a different level. But meeting as adult strangers, we are simply just another couple in love. I don't see where the taboo lies in having a consensual adult relationship when the biological connection is known after the fact. So from that viewpoint, we are a couple in love, and that's all I have to say."

Doris leaned back in her chair and looked hard at the two of them. The silence lasted a solid two minutes before she spoke.

"I know it's not ideal, but I believe your dedication to each other is true. It couldn't be anything else. So, I'm happy for you both but take care—no babies unless you adopt. Okay, I will not mention it again. But now for some news."

Doris had learned from her sources in the grand council that Snobby Pyles had left his old haunts, taking with him not only his family members—his wife, a daughter, and his mother-in-law—but also Pikey's wife and two children. Leaving in a great hurry, he sold off for cash all that he could sell in the way of property and Pikey's collection of Victorian ruby glass and gold jewellery. He also sold off all the stolen and fenced property in his lockups and even tried to sell to the girls in his brothels their own business. Needless to say, the last bit failed, and the girls thought that maybe they could keep the money they would earn without him. He was gone but without the finance that he thought he was worth. Hopefully, it would be the last anyone would hear of Snobby Pyles.

"Everard, you do know what this means, don't you? There is now a vacuum in that area of the East End, and it will likely give way to competition among the other gangs to take Snobby's pitch. We have two choices. Either we get in there and fight any opposition which could be risky to our presence in North London, or we could let them fight it out between themselves.

"There is also another problem to face and that is the police out there. So many of them are on the take that it's going to be difficult to find an honest copper, and we won't be starting at the top. There is one last option and that is to let them go their own way. If we worked on bringing in from the outside all those areas to the north, the south and east of the East End and made sure that the corruption couldn't leak out, then we might, in time, see a total collapse of the gangs through lack of finance. We would have to stop any people-trafficking and drug infiltration to start with and that would be something to really hurt them. What do you think?"

Everard at that moment realised that this was the opportunity that he needed to become more involved. He understood that Doris had at her fingertips no end of talents. He responded with some determination in his voice.

"Doris, I'll see what I can do to clear out the police situation. I'll get down to the local stations and accuse some of them of being involved in child abuse and protecting Snobby and his brother while getting paid for it as well. What I need is a couple of serious helpers to pose as Special Branch officers, that is if you can get us the necessary identification that we would need to be convincing.

"Also we will need a black Range Rover with shaded windows. Can you get me a rundown of the staff at the station from the detectives down to the beat constables and also any Masonic connections which the inspectors and local chief constable might have? As far as I know, if you turn the screws hard enough, there will be at least one person who will be honest and feel that the time is right to point a finger at those who are running all the rackets. Then we can move in as a force, round up the problem and give the others a chance to be genuine keepers of the peace."

"You are a crafty devil, aren't you, Everard? I know what you want. You want to get closer to the organisation and meet some of the activists, don't you?"

"So what's wrong with that? Look Doris, you said to me that it is about time that I started to get more involved. I can't get involved if I don't know who anybody is. I think that's reasonable, isn't it?"

Sarah had a look of serious consternation. "Are these people armed? If they are as corrupt as you say Doris, then Everard and whoever goes with him may end up in the mortuary, and I'm not sure if I could cope with that."

"Okay, Everard, I'll have a word with the council and tell them what you have suggested, and we will take it from there. I must say, taking control of the police and manning it with a bit of honesty is a good idea but will cause other problems in regard to the other gangs. There may be some blood flowing after this if the council agrees.

"I understand that we are still receiving some funds from the government. They still don't seem to have noticed that life has changed in this part of the world. They still think they are giving grants to the old town councils and only accuse us of not receipting those payments. Okay, when it comes to it, the civil service, clerical officers, and staff seem quite happy and have reported a considerable reduction in the workload since we took control, and our newly recruited police force is a proper force and not controlled by people itching for self-aggrandizement. Just as it should be. Right, Everard and you, Sarah, what are your plans?"

Sarah was quick to answer. "I think that the first step is for me and Everard to get married, just to start things on a proper footing."

Doris's face was a picture to see! It was if she had been swung through the air over the London Eye and had landed somewhere in the Thames.

"What! You can't do that! It's not … " She stopped midsentence when she realised that both Sarah and Everard were almost on their knees from laughing. "Don't ever say anything like that again! I might end up dying from a heart attack, and then, who would look after Molly?"

At that moment, Doris's telephone rang. There was a short silence while she took in the news.

"Well, that's a turn up!" she exclaimed. "Snobby Pyles is dead. Apparently, he'd gone off to Glasgow and tried to make contact with one of the drug gangs there, but all that happened was that he was set upon by a bunch of kids. According to a witness, one of the boys said, 'So you are the famous Snobby Pyles, are you?', walked up to him, stuck a knife up under his ribs, and that was that. The witness said that the kids just wandered off laughing, and one shouted, 'Good one, Skip!' So endeth another tale. I'm a bit shocked, though. I didn't think he'd be knocked off quite so soon."

Everard shook his head in disbelief. "I think Richie will not be unhappy about it, but it's a shame that crimes of that nature are now so rife amongst youngsters. Anyway, he's gone and that's that. We don't have to consider him anymore because he certainly won't be coming back."

Snobby had wanted Everard's skin to decorate his lounge, but fortunately, the threat was no longer valid, and Everard was happy to wear his skin a little bit longer, provided he resisted the temptation to beard another lion in its lair.

It was time for Molly's evening walk, and Doris thought that Everard and Sarah should do the honours while she prepared a meal. Molly was pleased to be with Everard, and deep inside, she hoped that once he was settled, she would be able to live with them. After all, she determined that Sarah was nice, and she was sure that Sarah would be quite happy to have Molly in her flat with Everard.

While the couple was strolling, Doris gleaned a little more intelligence from her informant. It seemed that the betting tax collected by the new state was not being forwarded, and the HRMC wanted to know why. They were told that there was no longer any betting allowed within the area and had at first accepted it. But now, those who ruled had declared that betting had to be reinstated because it was a major source of income for the treasury and therefore a necessity for the wellbeing of the National Health Service.

Doris had only a few words to say about it. "If it was up to me, I'd tell them to bugger off!" and she replaced the phone receiver, muttering to herself, "Bloody leeches! The bookies suck the punters dry and then the government wants its cut! Shocking ... shocking ... shocking!"

When Everard and Sarah returned, Doris had decided that a general meeting should be called with all the ruling members presenting a plan to fend off the intrusions of the state into the daily affairs of the new executive.

"Everard and Sarah, I've not been very forthcoming about my dealings and the way things are done. I am one of the founding members of the great council, and as such, I have quite a lot to do with the running of our programmes. It is now time for you to take a more positive position and act as a go-between with the state officials. We need some representation in parliament through the MPs who are meant to represent the various constituencies that we now run. As it stands, we have cleared out any local opposition in the council, schools, police, etcetera, but we now have to make our position clear to the state, which I don't think will be that easy."

She explained the situation with the Inland Revenue and clarified that if there was no gambling, then there would be no tax. The problem was that the HRMC seemed particularly fond of gambling as a major source of income.

"So what are you going to do about it, Everard? You instigated the situation when you got rid of those two obnoxious money lenders, and it was a really good thing to do. Just look at how far we've come since then!"

"God, Doris. Does that mean I'll now have to give up my job of doing nothing and get stuck into something that the state will call anarchy?"

"I'm afraid so, Everard. But you've got Sarah to fall back on when she's at home and not tending the sick. Chin up, Everard. I'm sure you can do it as long as you've got the will.

"By the way, I've heard that MI5 and Special Branch have got wind that we're ruling over North London. Apparently, we upset someone over a brown envelope that we confiscated, and they made a complaint to the chief constable in Birmingham, who then blew his little tin whistle. So we need to be careful not to kill too many MI5 operatives or Special Branch may start crying foul. I'll give them foul right up their ... " Doris looked at Everard hoping for a good response.

"How soon can you get everybody together, Doris? I can see that this might get a bit messy, and I'm not too sure of the way forward. Sarah, can you sit in and give me some ideas from your side of the table? It would be good to have a fresh look as to where we are."

"As long as it doesn't clash with my hours at the Royal Free. The thing is, Everard, this will interfere with any progress in the East End, and I'm sure nobody wants the gangs taking over Snobby's patch again." Sarah had replied almost reluctantly, feeling that the whole enterprise would fail if it was confronted by the weight of the government and its various nasty agencies, including the East End gangsters.

"I understand your concern, Sarah. I can see in your face that you have misgivings. It's odd that the government will always allow powerful mafia-type gangs to flourish under the umbrella of commerce but find it hard if not impossible to accept what we are doing and condemn it as anarchy. Just goes to show how democracy is so easily overrun by corruption and money.

"Doris, can you get a meeting set up by the day after tomorrow? I need to know who Sarah and I will be working with. Also, who is our controlling agent with contact to the local council offices? I can see there could be some serious discussion on the tax business. I don't even know how many people are involved in our circle."

"I'll see what I can do. By the way, I think that Richie should be involved because something else has cropped up regarding Snobby and his dealings with politicians. I was speaking to a journalist in the park the other day when I took Molly for a walk. He told me that there is a rumour that Snobby's death has left certain individuals in the Westminster government with a vacuum of a certain commodity, and we all know what that might be. Richie might have some answers and may be able to supply us with some ammunition.

"Anyway, leave it to me. But now, let's have dinner and put this aside for the moment. Molly, come along! Dinner is served!" Doris leaned over Molly and fastened a handkerchief around her neck as Molly jumped up to take her place at the dining table for the evening meal.

Chapter 10

The meeting left Everard, Sarah, and Richie feeling somewhat uneasy at first. There were just two of them, hooded in such a manner that it was impossible to make out precisely if they were human or not. It was a man and a woman as far as one could discern, who introduced themselves with curious pseudonyms.

Amanita Virosa, still clutching in her left hand a long-barrelled pistol modified to her own requirements, was the dead-eye markswoman responsible for the elimination of Pikey and Honeylicker's boys as well as several of the others. She said little and was as pale as death itself, visible only by the pallor of her near skeletal hands.

Standing beside her and leaning heavily on an old cane was Hector the Inspector as he called himself. He obviously suffered badly from Raynaud's disease since his hands seemed to drip profusely despite his clutching a rose-red handkerchief around the cane handle to quell the flow. Everard came to think that Hector may well have been the moderator of the council, but he couldn't be sure. His face, deeply hidden by the shadows cast by the hood of his long coat, gave little clue as to his age, but it emanated flashes from the extraordinary whiteness of his teeth when he spoke. His voice, though not loud, was of a pitch that every word was carried above all other sounds in perfect clarity. He was a large man, probably something over six feet in height with eight large, dark metal buckles holding his coat firmly together over his more than ample belly.

"Good evening, Everard. Good evening, Sarah, and good evening to you, my old friend, Doris. I trust that you are all well and sustaining your existence without grief. It is a pleasure that we have at last achieved the essence of our new estate, though I will say that the initial method of its inception may have been a little wayward."

Doris was quick to answer. "Well, it certainly got me out of a fix and many others too. Nonetheless, it was the start of a good thing, and I think we must all agree on that. Everard and Sarah, though there are only two here today, they do represent the wishes of the whole group, which may number several hundred by now.

"It is too dangerous for Hector to travel anywhere without the watchful eye of Amanita. She is completely focused on whatever problems might arise and deals with them without questioning. It seems a little cut and dry but is always effective and necessary to protect the validity of what we are all trying to achieve."

It was at this point that the doorbell rang, and Richie was ushered into the flat by an unseen hand. Hector was the first to greet him.

"Hello, young Richie! We have been dying to meet you. I trust that your burns are now quite healed. That was a nasty affair, wasn't it? But I can now affirm that the perpetrator of the attack is no longer with us, and his body was left for the dogs of Glasgow to feast upon. So endeth that part of the tale, but young Richie, there is something very serious that has occurred as a result of Snobby Pyles having been ejected from that part of the East End of London. It has left several MPs in the Houses of Parliament without their sordid forms of entertainment. I'm sure that you know as to what I refer, and we are very keen for you to apprise us of the actuality and participants of your generation who have been ostensibly servicing their debauchery."

Richie removed his coat, handed it to Doris, flopped down on her couch, and replied with far less verbosity. "From what you've just said, I gather that you want the low-down on the kids who the old sweetshop lady sent over to be shagged. Is that it?"

"Of course it is, Richie, and you have answered a delicate question with great aplomb. I'm sure that with your grasp on the situation, we will be able to move swiftly in order to protect these youngsters against any further misuse. Are you willing to guide us?"

Richie looked pleadingly to Sarah and whispered, "Is this guy for real?" Turning to Hector he replied, "Right, yeah. We'll sort it between us?"

"Indeed we will! Thank you, young man. I look forward to working with you. Firstly, could you make a list of all the youngsters who have become victims of these shysters? Secondly, we would appreciate details of their home backgrounds, how many other children there are in their families, how many have been taken into care in the past, and if they have any prior police records."

Richie had heard enough. "Just stop right there, will you? What do you think I am, some kind of bloody idiot? I can tell you who they are, but that is as far as it goes. I thought you wanted to hit the blokes who are using them, not sodding analyse if they were asking for it. Doris, can I have my coat? I'm out of here. Sorry Sarah, Everard, but this is out of my league. Can't you put him back in his box? Are you sure he's one of us and not some alien from outer space? He sure talks like one!"

Doris gave him his coat, and Everard called a taxi to take the youngster back to his parents. After the door had closed, Everard turned to address Hector.

"What the hell do you think you're doing? If this is the new estate, I think you can keep it. Up till now, I thought that there was sanity in the cause, but watching you has certainly caused me to think again. I thought you needed his help to sort this out. Now you've completely chucked it away!"

"Don't underestimate us, Everard, or you may have cause to regret it. Richie will talk, whether he likes it or not. He is in receipt of aid from us as are his parents, and we can simply put an end to it should he not cooperate."

Doris was too shocked and confused to react. She questioned what Hector had implied and thought to herself, *Do I really know this man? Have I made a mistake bringing him here?*

Everard clenched his fists at his sides, his eyes burning with anger.

Sensing that trouble was brewing, Sarah quietly edged herself behind Amanita. She felt sure that if a blow was struck, it would be up to her to keep Everard safe from a bullet or dagger from Amanita. Quietly, she grabbed a heavy vase on the sideboard behind her.

"Damn! I've just got stung!" Sarah shouted.

Amanita, turning quickly, was struck on the head so hard that she fell senseless against Hector. Being a true gentlemen with the benefit of a cavalier arrogance, he leaned away from his hapless comrade and let her fall to the floor. He looked down upon his protectress with a kind of disgust and brushed the sleeve of his coat as if it had been contaminated by the contact of Sarah's victim.

As he looked up, Everard hit him forcefully several times with an iron skillet, knocking the man senseless, a state that might well have been fatal. Blood spilled copiously from his split scalp with thin crimson rivulets beginning to flow onto the rug.

"Doris, what the hell are you doing messing around with this sort of filth!" Everard demanded. "This man's a creep of the worst type. This is not what we wanted! He's a leech just like those money lenders. I take it all the others are of the same mind. This group you're with seems to be just another type of Westminster government pretending to be for the people."

"I'm ever so sorry," Doris replied. "I'm just as disgusted as you are, and I'm ashamed that I allowed myself to be hoodwinked by these imposters. At least now we know that we can only trust each other."

Amanita had come to and looked up at the onlookers. Unscrambling herself and her thoughts, she sat up unsteadily. "I didn't even see that coming. Oh, and just look at him! Look at the state of the almighty warrior. Pathetic!"

Addressing Amanita, Doris inquired, "Okay, who the hell are you, really? And what's your stake in all of this?"

"Look, I need to say something first. I'm so sorry. I didn't want any of this to happen tonight and least of all what has gone on before tonight." Her voice was soft and mesmerising with an accent that Everard couldn't quite place. *Maybe Eastern European?* he wondered.

She continued, still in a daze. "In the beginning, I thought it was great, ridding the area of these parasites that have fed off the public for so long. It seemed right just to get rid of them, but then it all changed, and I found myself caught up being a bodyguard for people I didn't like or believe in." She paused for a moment, head bowed, then looking at them said, "I hope you'll give me a chance to prove myself."

She turned and gazed at Hector's prostrate body with contempt. "God, just look at him!" She leaned over Hector, clutched his windpipe between her bony index finger and thumb and squeezed. There was very little resistance, and within a minute, her one-time taskmaster had succumbed, gone off to meet his minions outside the gates of hell. Amanita raised herself back and sat cross-legged on the floor next to the body.

Everard and Sarah looked at each other, both shocked and bewildered. Seeing the consternation on their faces, Amanita said, "Don't worry yourselves about it. I'll take care of the mess."

Turning to Everard, "I have a confession to make. I've been following you. Whenever you were targeted, I got rid of the threat and you never knew it was me. I've been shadowing you for so long that I know the way you walk, your mood changes, your body language and what it conveys, everything about you."

"Why?" Everard asked. "Why me?"

"Ah, why you, indeed! I am a Roma from Bosnia, and my people have experienced the same political corruption but with a much more deplorable outcome. Perhaps someday I can tell you more. I observed what you did with the money lenders and the changes you tried to bring about. Your courage and determination touched me deeply, and it was clear that you were someone special that I needed to protect.

"Sarah, I was almost jealous when you came into the picture because I could not show myself whereas you had nothing to hide from.

"That monster lying there wanted me to report on everything that Everard did, and so I had to make up stuff, ordinary things like 'Everard went to the supermarket today' or 'Everard visited with Mrs. Wells,' and he'd write it all down in a little book. Look, there it is, sticking out of his pocket." She stretched over the corpse, slid the book out, and handed it to Everard.

"Look at it," she said. "He even had somebody watching Doris."

Doris returned from the kitchen struggling with a tray laden with a teapot, cups, little cakes with cherries on top, a bowl of chocolate biscuits, and the requisite milk and sugar.

"Well, that's a bloody turn up, isn't it!" she exclaimed as she plopped the tray down on her dining table. "Everard, dear, make yourself useful and pour it out for me. I need to call Richie to see if he made it back home alright. He was really pissed off by that creep, so I think he needs to know that the danger from that corner is now gone."

Doris wandered back into the kitchen, but returned almost at once. "Everard," she whispered, "Richie wants to talk to you. He says it's urgent and private." She handed her phone to Everard, leading him back into the kitchen.

"Is that you, Everard? Look, that geezer, I recognised his voice, you know—the words, the way he speaks. He's one of them that the old lady in the sweet shop used to talk to. He was often there for at least the last two years. I think he was the one who was getting the boys out to various places in London for that lot in Westminster. He's one of them, and the other one, Amanita, she's really scary. I saw it when she injected the skip driver. She just walked past the lorry, and it was like treading on a twig. A little jab and he was off with the birds. He didn't know where he was! She's so cool, but keep an eye on her. I don't know whether she's okay or not."

"Richie, listen to me. She just knocked mystery man off his perch, so don't worry about him anymore. She seems on the level and has already come up with a lot of details. I think you're quite safe now. I'll see you tomorrow and we'll all have a chat, Amanita as well. She could be a really good friend. I really believe that. I'll call you in the morning, okay? Take care, lad. Say hello to your mum and dad for me. See you tomorrow."

By the time Everard had finished speaking with Richie, Amanita had already drunk her tea, demolished three cakes and half of the biscuits.

Everard sat down beside her and slipped her hooded cape back over her shoulders, revealing her long, dark, wavy hair and piercing brown eyes. She was significantly younger than he had thought, maybe in her late twenties but with a hunger etched deeply across her face. The scar that ran across her right cheek was the only disfigurement of an otherwise beautiful woman, but even that was of no real value because Amanita's eyes were the only things that one would ever see. They absorbed everything and reflected everything upon which they settled.

She looked from one to the other as if expecting an attack, but Everard put his arm round her and gave her a reassuring hug.

Amanita took a deep breath, relaxed with a sigh of relief, and leaned her head against Everard's shoulder. She closed her eyes and fell immediately into a deep sleep. She was like a cat, lost in the wilderness for years, finally reaching home.

Chapter 11

When Amanita finally awoke, her head was resting on a pillow, and Everard and Sarah were gone. Doris set a fresh pot of tea on the coffee table and served two cups. "Here you are, dear. How do you feel?"

"Mostly tired with a bit of a headache. Thank you for your kind hospitality, Mrs. Wells. How long have I been out?"

"Oh, about three hours. And please call me Doris."

Amanita's eyes searched for the others, who were conspicuously missing. "Everard and Sarah … ?"

"They've gone back to the apartment to get some rest, but they'll be back in the morning. Everard will be arranging a meeting between Richie and us tomorrow to discuss the sordid details of meetups between boys and Westminster officials, apparently arranged through Hector. Speaking of which, he's still lying there making a right mess of my carpet. What should we do with him?"

Amanita arose from the sofa, looked at the pale corpse now showing signs of rigor mortis, and gave the body a hefty kick. "Bastard!" she muttered. She returned to the sofa and sat down in deep thought.

Finally, she spoke. "From the looks of him, we can make it appear like a hit and run but on somebody else's patch. I just remembered he's got an old Jensen in a lock-up. It's built like a tank and won't dent enough to arouse any suspicion if it doesn't get seen. I suppose if I was to prop him up with a stick in the road and then have a good run at him, it might look authentic. It'll have to be somewhere quite remote where he won't be found until he is really festering. Any ideas?"

Doris thought for a moment and recalled Everard's trick with Wragge.

"There's a place about three miles away. The back overlooks a vast overgrown field, and a lot of fly-tipping goes on there. It really stinks from what I've heard, so nobody will notice the stench of a corpse, especially if they're there to tip some junk illegally. Who's going to admit why they're there? I don't care for the idea of adding more garbage to a pile of rubbish out there, but it's a solution. I suppose we could build a bonfire somewhere, but that'll take more effort and may attract attention. I'll get the others to help you. Come on, let's get this bastard closer to the door."

***

Amanita was beginning to feel alive again and connected. The young woman had shed her hooded cloak, let her hair loose, and had a glimmer of colour returning to her skin. Overall, she was substantially more attractive, even as an assassin, than she had appeared in the company of the late Hector "the inspector" Plasma.

Doris was unable to quell her curiosity. "Amanita, my dear, where did you learn your skill? There aren't many who can do that kind of work and seem to be so unaffected by it."

"Oh, that!" came the almost casual response. "I don't really like to talk about it. It was down to my father and brother, both having been shot dead by Milošević's murderers who came to my village in Bosnia from Kosovo. They took them outside and made them dance while they shot at them, and when they were dead, the men came back inside and raped my mother in front of me, one after another, all eight of them. I was only fourteen years old. In the end, one took out a knife while the others held her down, and stabbed her three times in the stomach. I had been tied to a chair in such a way that I couldn't help but see what they were doing to my mother.

"They then turned to me and were just about to rape me as well, when there was a sudden series of shots, and the captain called for the men to take cover. I will always remember their words: 'Don't even think about running away, little girl. We will find you!' When they left, my mother managed to find just enough strength to loosen the rope around my wrists, and I was able to eventually slip out of the tie. She rolled onto her back exhausted and coughed. Her blood just gushed out of her mouth, and I knew there was nothing that I could do to save her."

Amanita paused, swiping a silent tear as if forbidding her pain from fracturing her stoicism.

"When the soldiers finally left the village, I started looking for dead ones, and eventually I found one. He must have been a sniper because his gun was not the usual Kalashnikov but a special rifle with telescopic sights and a few other modifications. So I took that and his ammunition and set about finding the people who were responsible for the murder of my family. I shot them all.

"I met other people from our village who had suffered the same fate. After a while, there were more from other villages who came to me for help. From then on, I made it my mission to eliminate the killers who were murdering my people. That is how I acquired my name—Amanita Virosa, the Destroying Angel—after that beautiful but deadly fungus.

"I was about sixteen when I finally made it to the UK as a refugee, and even then, I had a problem. As a Roma, I was not welcome in this country. I didn't know it at the time, otherwise I would have never come here. First the Nazis, then the Communist regime, after that the Serbs, and all we have ever done is mind our own business and try to keep to ourselves. The only ruler who ever stood by us was Tito. It's a shame that he died."

Amanita fumbled in her pocket and produced a small piece of blood-soaked cloth. "Look, this is all that I have left of my family. I cut this from my mother's tunic. That's all there is left." Amanita pressed it to her lips and stood silent remembering all that had happened. She put the cloth away and looked up with a smile. "Now, we had better get Hector into a bin bag, hadn't we?"

Doris held her breath trying to quell the intense grief that had welled up inside her. "My god, Amanita! I hope that sort of thing never happens again. How do you cope with it? I can't begin to imagine the horror that you must have endured! Such evil." It was almost too much for Doris to take in. "Amanita, dear, is that where the scar came from?"

Amanita laughed. "Ah, the heroine with a combat scar! Sadly, yes. I was only fifteen when some Serb soldiers came to my village and began to slaughter innocent people. I shot a group of them but then one came after me and slashed my face while trying to subdue me. I'm often asked about it, and I usually blame it on a terrified feral cat. Like I said, I don't like to talk about it, but it's a constant reminder of how far I've come."

***

Doris had phoned Everard early the next morning, and the scratching at the door by Molly announced his arrival.

"Hi, Doris! Sarah's on duty today so it's just Molly and me. Hello, Amanita! Gosh, you look so much better today." Everard had not noticed the pained look on Doris's face, which still bore the grief she felt after Amanita's story.

Amanita gave Everard a warm hug. "Everard, so nice to see you again! Yes, I'm feeling much better after a good night's rest. Doris was kind enough to let me sleep on her sofa last night."

"Where have you been staying?" Everard asked.

"Oh, here and there. I've preferred to not stay in one place. Makes it harder for people to find me though eventually I'd like to settle somewhere.

"Anyway, I've just been through Hector's pockets again and found a list of names in the lining behind his coat pocket. Look at this! Each name is countered by another, so we have Blundersly countered with Timothy, Grudgewick opposite Laurie, Fagham with Dicky and so on. To me this looks like a shopping list. We need to ask Richie if he knows any of them by just their Christian names."

Everard and Doris looked at the lists. There were two sheets altogether written in large red letters.

Doris gathered her thoughts, which up to that moment had been well and truly scattered. "Isn't this one a senior policeman? He was on the television two days ago talking about how vulnerable children are when they're in care. And look, this Buckleclip ... isn't that the bloke running the navy? Wouldn't forget a name like that, would you! My god, look at this lot. They're all in the Lords, the Justice, and the Church. I think this is seriously out of our league. We need some big-time help in this and some bloody good advice. I can see a death sentence if we're not too careful. Can you give Richie a call? See what he makes of all this. To me, this looks much the same as Dorkin's notebook when we first met up, Everard. It could be a blackmail list, even. I wonder how much he made out of this. But there again, after what Richie said ... "

Richie was having a home visit to check on his burns when Everard called but agreed through his parents to meet up at Doris's apartment the following morning.

"Everard, love, can I still follow you around or will it be a problem for you and Sarah. I'd hate to get between you, especially since you are so closely related."

It hadn't bothered Everard up to that point. As far as he was concerned, he was plainly in love with his sister, and so what.

Yet the attention that Amanita was showing was baffling but flattering. He was beginning to sense there was more than her desire to protect him. "Let's talk and figure out our roles when we come up with a plan."

***

The next morning, Richie entered Doris's apartment with an expression of intense curiosity. "Well! Where is the old bastard? I want to give him a bloody good kicking."

Amanita, who had been watching Everard's apparent discomfort, jumped up from the couch. "Come on over here, Richie. He's in the cupboard. Don't kick him too hard, though. He's stiff as a board. We're taking him for a ride later this evening to a place where he really belongs." She giggled a little at the thought of it as she took Richie's hand and led him over to a cupboard in the hallway.

"Go on, Richie!"

Richie replied, "You know, seeing him like that, I don't even want to get my boots dirty."

They all returned to the lounge where the list was offered to the youngster. He took a quick look at it. "All the names here are of the kids who disappeared from my old patch. They all went off at different times, and none of them ever came back.

"Look, this one, Timothy. He used to live right next door to me. I used to call him Chunky 'cause he was quite plump. He was really nice, and I liked him a lot. I remember him being pulled into a black Range Rover which turned up at the side of the playground. Mum called the police about it. I even gave them number on the plates, but nothing was ever done. Snobby's boys then turned his parents' house over and beat them up. That was about three years ago. Now I know what happened to the poor sod. Oh, I feel really awful, poor little guy. We got to get them! They got to pay for this! Oh, this is terrible! What are we going to do, Everard? What are we going to do about them?"

Everard was silent. Amanita was looking at him expectantly, waiting for an answer. She could see that he was in a real dilemma.

"Everard, there are about thirty names here. We don't need to know what has happened to those children because we already know. They're likely all dead. So all I need to know now is what these men look like. I'm sure I can find them, but I'm going to need some cover on this. I should think that after the first few are dealt with, the word will have gone out and the rest of them will be on their guard."

"Amanita, I know what you're saying, but this is going to be a lot bigger than just this lot here. Look, Snobby was just a go-between in a large operation. There are all those other gangsters up and down the country, in every big city, getting caught up in the same rackets, and we don't know who they are! If we knock off the names on this list, the rest of them will find out who's been doing the work, and they will not be happy about it. Losing money, that's all they ever think about.

"We need to stretch our wings and gain a lot more support before we embark on such a purge. Doris, who's not from this area in the council? Somebody who has that extra bit of credibility in another area. Do you know anybody? Amanita, I think if you knock off, say, four of those bastards in the beginning and then go to ground, we might stand a chance of getting a bit of respect, not quite sure from whom, but it could well happen. To go after the whole lot would be extremely dangerous."

Richie was frowning. "Where am I in all of this? Come on, I'm still under sixteen, still young enough to be bait, aren't I?"

He was met with silence. Richie had announced a game changer and had struck a very tender nerve in all of them.

"It's too dangerous, Richie, much too dangerous. But I'll bite. What are you actually thinking?" Doris regarded Richie with a look of intense interest and curiosity.

"Simple. Look, you've got the names and their addresses. Should be quite easy to find. Say I make myself visible around where they live. With a bit of luck, I should be spotted. When the target takes the bait and approaches, Amanita could make her move. That way I don't get touched, and the bloke pays the price for what he's done before. Now that Snobby's out of the way, these buggers must be getting quite hungry for little boys. I s'pose I'll have to go back to wearing short trousers for a bit. Mind you, it won't be so bad bearing in mind it's still not so cold now, but I won't be doing this in the winter snow, that's for sure."

Amanita laughed. "Action at last! When do we start, Richie?"

Everard and Doris looked at each other in amazement.

"Have you noticed, Everard, how much they react alike?" Doris enquired. "Must be that mischievous twinkle in their eyes. When Richie gets something in his mind, he has that same look, just like Amanita, sort of mischief mixed with devilry. God help us if this goes wrong!" Doris took a deep breath and sighed. "I think I'll go feed Molly now. She looks as puzzled as I feel. Come on, Molly! Sausages this morning."

Molly thought to herself, *About bloody time too! But that's the problem with being short ... one tends to get overlooked. Besides that, what's with all these sausages? Every day, sausages, sausages, sausages! What's wrong with dog food?*

Everard was worried. "I'm definitely not happy with this idea, Doris, with all due respect to Richie. There will be repercussions after the second one, so we need to find a friendly and honest voice who is in or around the government in one capacity or another. Someone who knows who to trust, someone like a straight policeman or even a decent politician, if that's even possible.

"Let's face it, though. The corruption in the system is so rampant that there are always those who will work to defend it. I can see this is going to be difficult, especially with the reaction in the press. *The Mail* and *Sun* will make out that the targets were all true pillars of society and demand instant retaliation against the 'communists' or some left-wing group. I can see the headlines now: 'Honest John murdered by far-left extremists supported by Russia.'"

Amanita had her own ideas. "Oh, Everard, sweetheart. It's really so simple. You're letting your mind wander into dark places. We've got the list, remember? I could probably do the lot in a fortnight. They can't be too difficult to take out. Look, the way I see it is that once they realise what's going on, the ones that remain will all go to ground. So if we act quickly, I could bag the lot before that happens, and that would be that. I can almost see the flag over Westminster flying at half-mast for at least a year!"

"One problem, Amanita. The regular police and their other agencies will be after us in no time. I really think it would be better to out them. The only way to do that is to find a sympathetic female peer, someone who has garnered a lot of respect, to name these people in the press. But we need to get loads of evidence without putting Richie in more danger than he has already encountered."

Amanita sat down. "Oh, Everard, my sweet, you are such a spoil sport! I was beginning to get excited, and now I feel really let down. Come over here," she said as she patted the cushion next to her on the couch.

Doris was amused watching Everard's face. He did not need Amanita's attention at that particular moment but still plopped himself down next to her. As luck would have it, the doorbell rang, and Sarah was ushered into the lounge by Doris. Molly was the first to greet her, but she did not miss Amanita removing her hand from the back of the couch close to Everard's neck.

"Hello, Amanita! So nice to see you again. Everard, will you take my bag? I've got some stuff in there for dinner. and there's a couple of bottles of wine in there as well."

Everard jumped up. "I've got it! Alison Quigley. She's the one. She'll do it!"

Sarah had no idea what the group had been discussing; "Who's Alison Quigley?"

Having gotten up, leaving Amanita gritting her teeth, Everard took Sarah's hand and led her into the kitchen. "Thank goodness you've arrived. Amanita is beginning to get too close. I don't know what to do."

Amanita had followed the couple and overheard Everard's remark to Sarah. "Simple, Everard! Just give in to her! Look, don't worry, you two. I'm just playing around. I'm going out now to find someone on the list. If I get lucky, I might find several of them together."

Everard and Sarah were speechless.

"I'll be back. Come on Richie. Work to do!"

***

It was early the next morning that the full horror of the story was broadcast on the BBC News.

Five MPs and two members of the House of Lords have been found dead, tied to the railings opposite the Houses of Parliament, each labelled with the name of a boy who has disappeared without a trace. Police are investigating how the perpetrator managed to parade the dead in such a manner without being seen. Nothing was visible on the CCTV in the area except a small boy throwing stones at ministers' limousines, something that may have attracted the attention of the police away from the stringing up of the victims to the railings.

During the days that followed, it had been noted that several official members of Parliament had resigned along with members of the judiciary, armed forces, and the police. The government was suddenly in disarray, with the prime minister declaring that it was not time for another general election despite having to preside over a very much diminished minority government.

As he anxiously tousled his hair trying to find words, the prime minister claimed that there was no problem and that it was just "a blip." He swiftly withheld any access to the corpses who had filled the mortuary in the crypt under St. John's Chapel.

But the parents whose children had vanished and been named on Hector's list demanded answers. One mother commented during a telecast interview, "If these men have been killed, surely somebody must know what had happened to our missing children." Most of the right-wing press was reluctant to follow the story, but too many questions had been raised in Parliament, and it became impossible to suppress any details that came to light regarding the escapades of the dead men.

Amanita and Richie had gone to ground, Richie as a student at the new school in which he had been enrolled and Amanita as a road sweeper.

Following an in-depth investigation by "Panorama," the BBC TV programme, evidence of the huge paedophilia ring within the halls of power was revealed with the obvious outcome being the prosecution and imprisonment of many of those participating in the ring. However, none were convicted of murder, most only receiving a slap on the wrist or being placed on the sex offender register. Amanita was appalled and absolutely furious.

"I risked a great deal in that mission. This is not what I wanted. There's going to be retaliation even if I am to die in the attempt."

In the days that followed, she realised that the only way to get justice for the youngsters was to make herself known, and she knew that it was the last thing she wanted to do. Calling in at Sarah's flat, she approached Everard and explained what she was about to do.

"Everard, I have arranged to have an interview on the television news the day after tomorrow. That interview will be my death sentence. Believe me, I know how it works. I will be branded as a terrorist by the government in order to cover up all the information that I will broadcast. They will tell the nation that I was a threat to democracy. As you know, they have their own definition of democracy.

"Everard, my love, as hard as I've tried not to reveal what I feel for you, I'm afraid I can't hold back any longer. The possibility of never seeing you again after the broadcast has given me the courage to tell you what I feel. Whether or not you feel anything for me is irrelevant now. I want you to kiss me, my love. It will be the last kiss that I shall ever receive because on Wednesday, I shall die. Kiss me now. I want to carry with me the taste of your lips and remember the sweetness in my last breath." She came closer and placed her arms around him.

Everard was overcome, not as much by her admission but more with the thought of losing her. "Amanita, please don't do this. Surely, there must be another way —"

Amanita placed her finger on his lips, then gently pressed her lips against his. He acquiesced, responding to the strength of her emotions and finality of her words. As they separated, Amanita wiped a tear from her eye, quickly turned and left the room. He called out her name, but she didn't, couldn't stop.

As she departed, she met Sarah on the stairs. "I'm sorry, Sarah, I can't talk now," and she scurried away, hardly able to control her tears.

Sarah found Everard sitting on their couch looking very gloomy.

"I just met Amanita on the stairway. She looked very upset. And now here you are, looking equally as miserable. What's happened? Have you had an argument or something?"

"No, but I don't think we will ever see Amanita again. She's embarked on a mission that will end in her death and she knows it." Everard explained all that Amanita had said to him.

Sarah thought for a moment. "We need to talk. As much as I appreciate Amanita's strength and willingness to help us, her flirtation with you is bothering me. What's going on, Everard? Do you have feelings for her too?"

He reached out for her, but Sarah moved away, crossing her arms.

"Sarah, surely you're aware of my love for you. I did think Amanita might have feelings for me, but I wasn't sure until now. I greatly admire her, but that's as far as my feelings go. You are my love. I want you to believe that. Come here."

Sarah gave in and fell into his arms.

As they held each other, Everard's mind went to Amanita and her revelation. He could still feel the touch of her lips and wondered, *Am I falling for her too?*

***

"Everard, Sarah, I'm so glad you came to see me. Amanita has been very quiet for the last couple of days and brooding over something that she didn't want to discuss. Your explanation makes it all clearer now. She needs to somehow survive that interview. I have some calls to make. I'm not sure what we can do at the moment, but I'll have a better idea in the morning, and we can discuss it then. Amanita is not the only one protecting our founding group. It's regrettable that Hector managed to get in among us. I'll bring that up as well. It's all a question of security. By the way, you know he was working for the Home Secretary. I'm surprised that he hasn't been missed by anyone there."

Doris made the call, and a plan was set based on assumptions of the way the government would probably react when under such a threat. The council knew that the government's main worry was that they would lose even more seats in Parliament, and any sacrifice was possible.

Amanita was unaware of the plans made by Doris and the council and made her television debut as arranged. As she entered the recently built New Broadcasting House, she was aware that she was, to say the least, a kind of celebrity. Even the viewing numbers for that evening were elevated far beyond the usual political interview. She refrained from the make-up and high heels. "I am here as I am. That is enough."

The interviewer began: "You have claimed that you are the assassin of five members of our Parliament though you have not registered this admission with the police. We are more than curious as to why you carried out the killings and have now come to us to admit your guilt."

The interviewer was obviously disbelieving that Amanita was responsible for what had taken place. "And who was the young lad who made the diversion, giving you time to attach your victims to the railings outside the Houses of Parliament? You must have had several accomplices to carry out such a feat."

"I have not come here to divulge the identities of any accomplices that may or may not exist. I have come to explain the reasons behind my determination to alert the public as to the kind of people who now represent and even lead many of the governmental posts, and not just in the government, but also in the police, military, and judiciary. These people are responsible for deaths under horrific circumstances in order to satisfy their vile lust.

"Firstly, I have in my possession a blackmailer's list of names, each of which is opposite the name of a youngster who has been registered as missing. Some of the children have been gone without a trace for several years. This list came into my possession by chance, having found it in the pocket of an ex-member of the Home Office. He was the procurer of young flesh for these individuals, children taken or lured from the East End in an area run by the gangster Snobby Pyles and his brother, Pikey. Both these men, now dead, meant to fulfil the lust of those perpetrators through enquiries made for a new source of supply. This list was found in the pocket of their envoy.

"My quest is far from finished, but I fear that this submission is also the acceptance of my death sentence because there are far too many in high office that need to put an end to my life and, by that, securing their own anonymity. I want the viewers to know who is likely responsible should my sudden demise come to pass."

Without giving the interviewer a chance to question her further, Amanita rose and strode out of the studio and descended the stairs to whatever punishment awaited her. At the door, she hesitated for a second, and then removing her coat, she offered herself to the killers that she knew would be waiting.

The first shot hit her in her left thigh, the second in her abdomen, and the third missed, ricocheting and smacking into the glass entrance door. Several other shots followed, but they were no longer fired in her direction. Two bodies were dragged into view of the CCTV cameras and dumped in full view of the journalists, who were already snapping images of whatever was possible to see.

The outer courtyard of the building began to fill with hundreds of people as Amanita's body was carried away to the mortuary. The news studio was unprepared for what was to happen next. The attempt by the government at shutting down the service had failed as the whole building had now become subject to the rule of the new order. Interviewers stood mutely as a spokesperson addressed the viewing public.

"You have seen tonight the manner in which the government, your government, deals with people who try to protect your children from the abuse of those who are supposed to protect your interests. Tonight you saw the assassination of a young woman who, through her own courage and bravery, sought to eliminate some of the vilest people, people in elevated positions, people who are party to and guilty of murdering your children.

"We have evidence that the two assassins are directly connected to the Home Office and under orders from cabinet ministers. These two men are, by their credentials, members of the government's police protection force. They have paid the ultimate price for the crimes that others committed.

"We are the new order, originally formed in North London, and have peacefully run a happy and productive community where all needs have been met regardless of government policy. The government has failed to even be aware that this area, consisting of nearly two million people, has been detached from its rule. We have helped all those in need, found homes for the homeless, fed all those who are without, and rid the area of debt and pernicious addictions. This has been achieved painlessly for the public, the only victims being those who propagated corruption and lived off its proceeds.

"We propose to you, the public of this island, to follow our example and create a new form of government from commune to commune, with a general council to gather all your thoughts and desires, to discuss the way forward and forever rid us of this disgrace that has been festering for generations under our very noses.

"Talk among yourselves. Come to us with your ideas if you want to follow our example or gain further information. It is achievable. We leave it to you to choose. In the meantime, we will continue to run this service and will keep you updated with any further news from the world around you. That will not change. Good luck to you all."

It was at this point that another broadcast commenced listing the names of all the perpetrators in Parliament, the judiciary, and the armed forces responsible for the deaths and incarceration of so many of the young disappeared.

The following day, the government, having spent a sleepless night discussing the way forward, eventually chose the "suicide" argument. The prime minister addressed the nation on Sky, having no longer access to the BBC.

"Owing to the great stress and difficulty that the senior MPs listed yesterday on the other broadcasting stations suffer in carrying out their duties of representing the public, keeping that public safe and the economy sound, they deserve the right to pass any free time that they might have indulging in whatever practice they wish. If any members of the public are harmed in these politicians' pursuits, it is lamentable but should not be considered as any kind of wrongdoing and as an expression of their love for the younger generations. This applies also to any of the senior and, for that matter, any junior members among our lawmakers, armed forces and those who make judgments to keep us safe.

"It is unfortunate that the poor, deranged young woman was eliminated yesterday, but it was a matter of necessity. If creatures like her are allowed to make their own judgments and sentences, then they will be put down. Armed forces are at this time removing those who briefly took over the airwaves, the National Broadcasting System. The status quo will be restored before nightfall, and you will be able to sleep with the understanding that we are keeping you safe from this insurrection. Thank you."

Indeed, a platoon of armed soldiers had arrived at Broadcasting House but were immediately disarmed without a shot being fired. They had heard the prime minister's declaration and were surprised that they were called in to protect what had blatantly shown itself to be a corrupt government. The soldiers were taken to a refreshment tent, given hot soup and fresh bread by a group of the forgiving residents of North London.

The perceived failure of their mission further aggravated the government, but the full significance of the prime minister's broadcast had horrified the nation, and any move to eliminate that aggravation became totally impotent. A crowd of several thousand angry citizens gathered in Hyde Park determined to put an end to the prime minister's "status quo."

Messages of support for the rebellion arrived from all over the country, giving the protesters a greater desire for the dissolution of the existing parliamentary system. Downing Street was now a target, particularly No. 10, and before the morning was out, the street was jammed with protesters. The police were totally outnumbered despite shots being fired into the crowd. Those injured or killed were carried away, which gave even greater impetus to the gathering.

Before long, a battering ram was brought into the street carried by twenty able protesters, and within another half hour, the doors of several of the governmental offices lay smashed within the hallways of the various buildings. Silence was the most noticeable and threatening element that then confronted the occupants. There was a long hush lasting a solid three minutes. Then a lone voice, clear and decisive, gave instructions for all ancillary personnel within those offices to leave. All ministers, political advisers, and political secretaries were ordered to await interrogation. All others were given thirty minutes to vacate those premises.

"It is 2:30 p.m. You have until three o'clock to leave," was the final demand. Cleaners and office workers were soon filing out through the broken portals and given clear passage through the gathering out into Whitehall. Every now and again, a politician masquerading in work clothes was seized and escorted back into the buildings.

At three o'clock, the same voice called again. "All other occupants of these offices must now show yourselves. We have a list of names associated with those mentioned on the television yesterday evening. The people thus recorded will be taken for trial by a National Public Court if an interrogation finds evidence in their testimonies that needs to be judged by the common people. We the people will cast our judgement upon them and not in one of their courts ruled by their own."

In a last-ditch attempt, the prime minister stepped out to address the crowd. "Go home now. You have been misled ... "

"We have been misled by your lot for years! For generation upon generation, we have listened to your lies and half-truths, and what has happened as a result? Poverty, poverty and more poverty! That's all you deal in!"

The response was furious. The leader of the state quickly drew back, realising that the world in Whitehall had now ceased to exist.

"I demand safe passage for myself and a couple of ministers. You can have the rest to do with them what you will!" he called out. "I am still your prime minister. I went to Eton and won the election, and therefore, I have a right to rule you riff-raff!"

At this point, a large metal cage strapped to the flatbed of a lorry was seen to slowly move up among the demonstrators. The prime minister shrank back in terror.

"You're all mad, totally insane! Go away, all of you! Leave me alone! Go away, go away. I demand it!" His words tumbled onto deaf ears.

It was now all too late for him. Every member of the cabinet was escorted to the cage, including the prime minister. Once filled, the lorry moved slowly out of Downing Street en route to Southampton and the prison ship that would take them beyond the Isle of Wight.

It was at that moment that a particularly enraged adviser to the prime minister lunged into view from No. 10 brandishing a machete. He rushed into the crowd of onlookers and attacked anyone who stood in his way. Finally being overpowered by members of the crowd, he was bound, gagged and strung upside down by his ankles from a lamppost outside the government offices. The crowd remained silent as they filed past him and out of Downing Street.

His fate was not of immediate interest. Only one thought filled almost every mind: *What happens now?* Reassurance was a necessity that the leaders of the coup understood and needed to administer promptly in order to calm the populace.

A spokesperson for the revolution stepped forward. "During the last twenty-four hours, we have delegated representatives in all parts of the country. They will help you form new councils, no longer along party lines but selected by you to democratically represent your views, address your concerns and be on your side to create a better country for your regional administrations. Your problems will be resolved and your fears dispersed. In the morning, we will broadcast the addresses of all the centres throughout the land where you may consult with our representatives. All information will be found in bulletins issued from various agencies during the course of the next few weeks and will also be available in broadsheets free of charge at railway stations throughout the land."

"As if it was that simple," was the attitude of those who seemed quite happy with what had existed. "Give it a day or two and then it will all go back to what it was, and all these idiots will be rounded up and put away for a good long time!"

But it couldn't go back. Nobody in the Houses of Parliament knew who would be next to be carried away in a cage. Even the most arrogant and outspoken MPs hid themselves lest their own crimes should come to light. Courts were already up and running, dealing with previously ignored injustices. Refuges for those in need, previously closed due to lack of government support, were once again opened. Food for the needy became more accessible, and the rich were given an ultimatum to either support the new system or leave the country. If they chose the latter, their accessible funds and property would be restored to the state and used in a manner to help the many and not the few.

On investigation into the funds that the old government had kept secret, it appeared that £23bn over and above what had been declared was available to push forward the plans of the new order.

Everard and Sarah were astonished at the sudden turn of events and were even more surprised when Doris appeared on television as the founding member of the new order.

"One of the great things about all of this is that with the money we save from not having the two Houses of Parliament, the members and their expenses, we will be able to fund the health service with an extra £350m per week. Rents in the private sector will be regulated to whatever level of income the tenants can afford. Nobody will be evicted for being poor."

Doris continued her mini-budget statement without interruption from the interviewer. "None of this would have been possible if it wasn't for the goodwill of a young man, a victim of a loan shark, who raised sufficient funds for me and many other OAPs who found themselves without heat or food during the cold weather.

"All of us were victims of a regime that allowed deceitful pay-day loans to flourish and landlords to evict at will any family that was unable to find sufficient funds to pay their outrageous rents. All this is now coming to an end! Nobody in the public sector need worry about their jobs. In that respect everything will continue, but there will be changes in many of the unsafe and unfair contracts that the previous administration had peddled.

"This is just the beginning. We will broadcast every change that we feel necessary and carefully consider public opinion and take advice from those qualified to give it. Everybody must look to a brighter future, but there is going to be much work to do clearing away the vestiges of the old regime. We all need your support as we go forward."

The private armies armed with weapons accessed from army barracks throughout the country willingly surrendered them on the orders of dissenting officers. Many supporters and activists of the new regime were gunned down, some beaten to death and others sexually abused in such a manner as to leave them with life changing disabilities. But that is the nature of some determined to desperately uphold an old, corrupt system and their own position within it, whether looking up from the bottom or looking down from the top.

Needless to say, those guilty were eventually all rounded up and paid out in full according to their crimes against the populace, though their families thereafter remained the responsibility of the state if they were left in need. There was no space in the new world, the new England, for dissent of that kind. Free speech was still respected but violence was restricted only to the people's judiciary. Gradually it was realised that there were so many benefits to be gained by just working together and not against each other.

The clean-up was thorough but took a long time to spread throughout the land. Eventually people became eager for the areas in which they lived to accept what they saw as being an amity and prosperity between all sections of the public, something that they had never seen before. The only real problem was recruiting enough politically aware activists to bring about the harmony that everybody (with few exceptions) wanted.

Finally, it was achieved. The new Britain was real. But for how long? Some people live only to luxuriate in the misery of others, and unfortunately, they too often thrive. Those elements when gathered together are most dangerous for democracy because it always threatens its existence.

Though the old government was essentially subverted, its avid adherents plotted and subtly reinforced those elements of state that had always utilised fear as a way to regain power. Over time, the new regime became complacent and failed to see and ultimately comprehend that its days were to be short-lived. The public dreamed on unaware of the knot tightening around their necks.

Chapter 12

It was sometime after Amanita was gunned down that Everard and Sarah, having become settled in each other's ways, were surprised to receive a call at the door of their apartment late one Sunday evening. Molly rushed to the door, barking excitedly in expectation. Everard rose to answer the door. He felt reassured that Molly was excited enough not to worry as to who might be knocking.

"Hello, Everard! I hope it's not too late for you and Sarah."

"No, no, Doris. Of course not. Come in, come in!" Everard had not noticed the shadow that lurked behind her.

"Hello, Everard. Lovely to see you again. I have missed you, you know. I hope I'm not intruding."

"Amanita! My god, we thought you were dead and that you had been buried in secrecy. What has happened? Come in, both of you. Sarah, it's Doris and Amanita! What a surprise!"

Sarah greeted them cordially, offered them both room to sit on the sofa and handed each a glass of wine. Molly was already licking Doris's hand as Everard and Sarah looked at each other in disbelief.

"Well, this is such a surprise! I don't know what to say. Amanita, what happened to you? You've been gone for months!" Everard blurted.

"Well, I was shot twice, but the one in my abdomen was the worst. That nearly killed me ... I can't do this anymore. I've lost my nerve. It's not having been shot but something else. I can't explain it, but I need to stop. Taking lives, no matter how much those monsters need to die, is no longer a choice that I can make. I've done enough, and I don't think that you need me anymore. Maybe I'll get a job somewhere, something to ease me away from my nightmares."

Everard stood as if in a trance. "Amanita, have you got anywhere to stay at the moment?"

"Yes, Doris kindly let me stay on her sofa after I was discharged."

"I think you need to have constant company for a while. So if Doris is busy then feel free to stay here. Sarah and I would be glad to keep you company. Besides, I owe you my life. Without you, somebody would have bumped me off ages ago."

Sarah did a double take, feeling incredulous that Everard had made such an offer without consulting her.

"True! Three times altogether. Thank you, Everard, but I need to speak to Sarah alone."

The two young women arose and left the room.

When they were out of earshot, Doris spoke her mind. "Everard, what are you thinking? Amanita is in love with you, and if she stays here, it will inevitably cause a rift between you and Sarah. I know I still feel uneasy about Sarah being your sister, and that is your business, but it also creates a double problem. If Amanita becomes a temptation for you, then Sarah will pick up on it, and you could lose two loves in one—your lover and your sister. Do you know what you're doing?"

"Not really," was all that Everard could say.

"She will have to stay with me. It's the only answer. I'm sure I can find her a job where she will have plenty of good company and where nobody knows anything of her past. I think it will be the best option. I'd hate to see any kind of animosity rise up between Sarah and Amanita. It would hurt all of us."

Everard took a sip of his wine, deep in thought.

***

Sarah and Amanita sat opposite each other in Sarah's bedroom.

"Sarah, this is very awkward for me as it must be for you. I suppose you know that I have feelings for Everard, and as much as I've tried to respect your relationship, unusual as it may be, I can't help what I feel. I think you're very beautiful and have such a kind heart. I'm wondering if there's any way that we can come to a compromise."

Sarah thought for a moment. "You know, Amanita, I too think that you're very attractive, and I really admire your character and your grit. In many ways, I wish I was more like you. I suppose that my jealousy comes from the feeling that Everard might think more of you than he does of me. The fact remains that he's my brother, and if anything were to transpire, he and I would always be connected. Could you live with that? How can we resolve this?"

Amanita reached out and held Sarah's hands. "Sarah, as open-minded women, I hope that you can consider what I'm about to say." She continued hesitatingly. "Could we live together, sleep together, love each other freely in our own ways? We could learn so much from each other and work closer together. I'm open-minded enough to accept that loving relationships can take many forms, much like you and Everard have chosen to love each other despite being siblings. Of course, it's important that Everard knows, understands, and accepts us being an intimate part of each other. Can *you* live with that?"

"It might work out well though I must admit that this is all new to me. We could give it a try and see where it goes."

"Great!" Amanita said. Let's discuss it with Everard."

They both stood and warmly hugged.

***

"Doris, Everard is my brother, and though you may find it difficult to accept us living as a couple, I trust that Everard and Amanita can work out their roles in what some would see as a ménage à trois. It is probably difficult for anybody to imagine that I might be quite happy to see him in an alternate relationship, but being his sister, I could possibly have an entirely different view. I'm sure we can all live together quite happily."

Doris took a deep breath. "Devil take you three. Far be it for me to understand these new-fangled relationships. Molly what do you think? D'you still want to stay here with these mad people?"

Molly smiled. She fetched her lead and presented it to Doris. "Come on, Doris. Walkies!"

"Goodness, Doris! Sometimes I think that your Molly can actually talk," exclaimed Amanita.

"Oh, but she can," she responded laughing. "Won't be long!"

Despite the darkness and the rain, Doris and her canine friend ventured out into the cold night air.

Those were the last words that Everard, Sarah, and Amanita would ever hear from Doris. Despite their desperate search throughout that part of London, no sign, no CCT footage. Nothing gave any clue as to what had happened to them.

Richie was devasted. Doris had been like a grandmother to him. Amanita was furious but felt, after her injury, oddly incapable to face what she really wanted to do. Everard and Sarah gave them both a refuge and shared their grief as best they could.

Within a couple of days, Richie and Amanita joined forces.

"We know what sort of people took Doris and Molly," Amanita remarked. "We don't have their names, but we know the type. We will hunt down their kidnappers, and we will try to find what remains, if anything, of Doris and Molly." Both Amanita and her understudy were of the same mind.

Amanita realised that her retirement would have to be delayed, and though she may have lost her nerve, it was not long before her grief and anger reprimed the feeling for revenge. Although it wasn't the same grief that she had known as a youngster, the loss of Doris and her affection for Molly were enough to focus her attention on those who perpetrated their disappearance.

She exercised every day and practiced several of the skills that had made her a force to be reckoned with. She took to wearing her signature dark clothing once more, which in the shadows and at night made her almost invisible. She oiled her guns, sharpened her knives and bought a good swordstick from an unknowing assistant in an east coast charity shop.

Richie ducked his schooling in order to seek out any information that he could from the kids all over North and East London. His taxi fares and meals were funded by the new order, and the information that he acquired gave him a greater understanding of the opposition that was gradually building against it. Corruption could never be stopped. It has always been part of the human condition.

Richie continued to circulate under the watchful eye of Amanita. She was never out of sight, but neither was she visible to the casual glance.

It was at a second visit to a small park in Tottenham that Richie was approached by a child no more than ten years old. "Are you still looking for your dog, mate?"

Richie affirmed that he was as the youngster fished out of his pocket a brass disc with the name *Molly* engraved on it. "Would this be anything to do with it?" young Kevin asked.

"Oh, bloody hell! Where in God's name did you get this?" Richie gasped as he clutched the little piece of metal. He knew that in his hand was the first part of a grim story.

"It was in the ashes of the fire. They burned them, both of them. The old lady was alive up till about three days ago. We could see her at the top window over there, the one with bars across it. She looked awful, but none of us dared go to the police or anything 'cause we knew that it was a government job. It always is when they've got someone up there.

"Sometimes we could hear her scream like she was being tortured, but I think she held out because she was in there for so long. Anyway, when they had finished with her, they burned the both of them. The dog was already dead though. You could see it. It was all stiff like an old teddy bear. Then with them on top of pallets, they threw on there what smelled like car oil and put a match to it, right in the middle of the road. It melted the tarmac as well.

"Look, it was just over there, near the letter box. Smoke got in all the houses. The smell of it made all of us really sick. You could see the bodies in the flames.

"The executioner shouted that if anybody wanted to stand up against them, then they would get the same medicine. But I've seen them. They've done it before. They did it to a woman who was living with a Black guy. We never saw him again neither.

"If you want to know more, the bloke who lives in that house over there is the one who builds up the fire for them, and he stands next to them when they do what they do. He cheers them on when the flames go up. It's number 43, but don't let him see you lookin' 'cause I don't want to end up like those others.

"Oh yeah, there's another thing. I've seen him taking stuff into the pawnbrokers on the high street. He's always got a bagful, so I reckon he fences it all away for the other lot. But watch out. Look! He's coming out now and he's looking over here. Don't say nothing that we've talked about if he comes over. Oops … here we go!

"Hello Mr. Green! All right?"

"Who's he? Come on, who are you?"

Richie was quick, "I'm his second cousin. Why? What's it to you? Are you the big chief round here or just a fat man sticking his nose into other people's business?"

"Is he for real, your cousin? Does he know who I am? Cheeky bloody mutt! Go 'orn, piss off back to your hole, you little shit!"

Richie was reassured by the appearance of a little red dot which hovered around the middle of the man's forehead. He smiled to himself as it gradually moved down a few inches below the navel.

"You should watch yourself, Mister! I can put you down quicker than you can think."

The reaction was almost funny as the oaf took a swing at Richie and missed.

"Come on! You'll have to do better than that!" Richie laughed, which enraged his opponent even more. Another assault followed, as futile as the first. But now the man took out a knife from his belt, then fell to the ground stone dead.

The young boy looked in amazement at Richie. "Christ! How the hell did you do that? Are you a wizard or what? I never saw you move! Bloody hell, I better get out of here before someone sees us. Keep the name tag, mate! I don't want it!" and the youngster scuttled away bent double as if creeping out of sight.

***

Everard listened carefully to what Richie had been told. He flopped down on the couch, his head in his hands. It was as much as he could do to hold back his tears. *Doris ... Molly, I'm so sorry!* It was too painful to dwell on, unable to fathom life without them. But in a way, he had half expected something to happen to ruin what had been a relatively peaceful revolution.

Sarah couldn't contain her sorrow and disappeared into their bedroom.

Shortly after, Richie thought it would be a good idea to return to his parents, and as he was leaving, he let Amanita into the apartment.

"So you've heard," said Amanita, "I don't know what to say, but I know what I want to do. I think our clean-up has not been very successful. I have a feeling that all this is going to end very badly. Everard, this has not happened by chance. This has been organised by agents of the old government, but I expect that you've already figured that out. Those cabinet members who were incarcerated must have been freed by somebody.

"Obviously, they still have a good deal of power whether we like it or not. These people will never rule by democracy because corruption is their way of life, and unfortunately, they will always prevail. They have the money, they have MI5, MI6, Special Branch, the army and its leaders all under their command, and that is why Doris and Molly have been murdered. No other reason. Trouble is, Everard, I don't know how we can fight them. The odds are against us. But if we don't fight it, we lose anyway, and they'll pick us off one by one. All we can do is fight on till the end. Where's Sarah? She should be here."

Sarah had heard what Amanita said and returned to the lounge. "What have you got in mind, Amanita? If your assessment of the situation is correct, I know that our time is soon to be up. So we need to do something if only to avenge Doris and Molly. I can't believe the old state has done this, but when I think about it, who are we in their scheme of things? We are no more than a grating headache, easily got rid of with a couple of paracetamol slugs."

Everard was scratching his head, deep in thought. He was now confronted with not only losing his own life, which he was quite content to do, but also with the responsibility for the death of a very brave woman who he not only loved but considered above those in power.

Suddenly, he shouted, "The pawnbroker! That's where we start! Doris always wore a gold brooch in the shape of an open book. Do you remember it? It was always on the right side of her coat. If he's got that, then he's probably in possession of anything else that she had with her. Amanita, I'd like you to hit him when he makes a run for it. Sarah and I will squeeze out of him the names of his suppliers, and then we will deal with them."

Amanita was quiet for a moment, then spoke up. "Everard, this smacks of a government plot. It could be that this is all to draw us out into the open, and then they will make an example of us before we have a chance to tell anyone about Doris and Molly. I've seen it before. It's a classic MI5 setup. We need to be far less visible in one respect, but more assertive in the other.

"Look, he deals in stolen property. That is where we need to get him. Draw him in and then draw him out if you see what I mean. I suggest that Sarah tell him that her aunt has just died, that she's been cut out of the will, and that the house is full of jewellery. If she gives him Doris's address, he's bound to attempt a break-in with some of his associates. It is there that we will wait for them. You do still have a key to her apartment, don't you, Everard?"

Everard dug in his pocket and held up the front-door key to Doris's apartment. "Let's do it!" he shouted. It was a side of Everard that none of them had seen before. He had become visibly agitated by Richie's discovery and would have fought with a bear while in his current frame of mind.

Sarah put her arm round his waist and whispered, "Focus, Everard. Focus! Remember we will all need to be cool-headed, and it's not going to happen without blood being shed." She tenderly kissed him on the cheek. "Take a deep breath and calm down. I'm sure Doris and Molly would not like us to join them for the sake of being too hasty, would they?"

***

It was on a Tuesday night around two in the morning that the burglary finally took place. Four men, including the pawnbroker, cut out a section of glass from the front door of Doris's apartment, released the door catches, and quietly entered. It was obvious that they were well prepared for the break-in.

Amanita noticed that three had guns. She identified the pawnbroker, his being the largest of the four particularly around the middle. She quickly dispatched the three who had separated from the main target — the first with her knife thrown from behind the bathroom door, the second and third with bullets to their heads from her silenced pistol.

The pawnbroker had no idea he was now alone but assumed that his comrades were a little clumsy working in the dark. He continued to whisper to them, "Come on, you lot! She said the stuff is all in the bedroom."

The beam from his torch scanned the walls until it settled on Doris's bedroom door. Sarah was waiting in the bedroom and could see the door slowly opening with the light from the torch making the fat man an easy target for Amanita. This time, killing was not a choice. The rope stretched across the room a few inches above the floor was sure to bring the man to his knees. Everard waited for the rope to meet the ankles of the thief, and with a gentle push, brought the fat burglar into a position from which he found it difficult to escape.

Amanita put her pistol to his head and said quietly to Sarah, "Shall I do it now or do you want to play with him for a little while before I put him down?"

Sarah stood over him and delivered a precisely aimed kick between his spreadeagled thighs. The pawnbroker screamed and writhed in agony on the floor.

When the pawnbroker calmed down a bit, still moaning with tears flowing down his cheeks, Everard held out his hand as if to help him up onto his feet. As the man reached out, Everard delivered a shake with such force that the right arm of the burglar was dislocated at the shoulder. Again, a tortured wail escaped from the rotund heister. It became clear to him that unmerciful pain was on the menu, and his death was there, waiting in the shadows of the room.

"Why did you do it?" Everard asked him in a calm, dispassionate voice.

"What? I don't know what you're talking about. Do what? For god's sake, do what?"

"Kill my mother and my dog? Burn them. Who was with you?"

"I can't tell you. I wasn't even there! They'll kill me if I give you their names!"

Amanita reacted. "We'll kill *you* if you don't! You have three seconds to make up your mind. One ... two ... " She had put the gun to the frightened man's head once again, but now holding the pistol in her right hand, she slowly drew a cut-throat razor from her belt with her left. Flicking it open, she slowly pared the hair from his right eyebrow, causing the pawnbroker to scream in terror. The game was up.

"It was a government contract to kill them," he said, his voice shaking. "They do it all the time. One of them comes by and tells Bertie Suggs who they want done and how to dispose of the victim. Bertie and his boys caught the old lady in the street one night, knocked her on the head, killed the dog right there beside her, and made off back to their pad with her and the dead dog in the van. Nobody saw them that would say anything. That's the way it's done around here.

"They told me what they had done and told me to get a big fire ready in the street for a barbecue in a couple of days and that they would give me the word when to get it started. I didn't want anything to do with it, so I asked Ferky the Greek to do the fire for me, and he did. It was him and his chum, Collard Green, who I think was knocked off the other day.

"I didn't know they were going to kill her. They didn't tell me that. But I can tell you who the bloke from the government is. His name is Boris Jenkins. He's bonkers. That's why he goes to Bertie Suggs because Bertie's bonkers as well and this Boris drinks in Bertie's bar every Thursday night. Most times he wants a little girl to play around with and Bertie gets him one.

"Look, I'm scared stiff knowing what they'll do to me if I ever stopped working for them. Looks like I'm between a rock and a hard place now. What are you going to do to me? You know, I didn't ask for any of this. I'm just a pawnbroker, and I thought it was an easy way to make some money. I didn't expect getting involved in all this stuff. You've got to believe me!" There was a general silence in the room as they all looked at the terrified man literally cowering at their feet.

Everard finally spoke in a manner that filled the man with even greater terror. "What do you think? Shall we let him go or build a good fire for him, or do you think it would be better to let fate take a hand and toss a coin? What's it to be, the gates of hell or a breath of fresh air? Sarah, Amanita, heads or tails?"

Three cornered coins never work. Amanita called heads and Sarah called tails as Everard tossed the 10-pence piece towards the ceiling. It was an impasse long before the coin had even landed. As they watched, it hit the ground and rolled out of sight between two floorboards. The three laughed.

Amanita looked seriously at the pawnbroker, whose sweat was now running in rivulets from the top of his head, down either side of his nose, leaving a large wet patch on the tee-shirt that barely covered his belly.

"Well, ain't that a bloody shame!" she growled. Everard and Sarah could barely stop themselves from laughing, but Sarah cut in with a suggestion.

"Shall we pinch a boat down at Eel Pie Island, shove some sticks in it and half a gallon of paraffin, and give him a warm send-off down the Thames?"

The pawnbroker finally succumbed to his all-consuming fear and slumped sideways unconscious. A sudden and rather loud knock on the door to the apartment brought them all to a standstill.

"Quick! Get him out of sight!" Amanita whispered, and the three dragged the pawnbroker towards the kitchen. "I'll stay in here in case he comes to."

Everard opened the door slowly, half expecting some kind of trouble, but instead, he was confronted by a slender young man.

"Are you Everard?" he asked. Hardly waiting for a response, he continued. "My name is Reuben. I was given this address by a mutual friend. I believe that I can be of some service to you. I recently heard that Doris and her dog had been murdered. I have some information as to the perpetrators of that crime and know of the agents who ordered their deaths. May I come in? I won't stay long."

Everard showed him into the lounge where Sarah suggested that they might all have a glass of wine. Everard nodded but barely looked away from this neatly presented newcomer.

"Where are you from and who exactly gave you this address?"

"Well, I'm from No. 10, and I got your address from an old lady who used to share a park bench with Doris when Doris took her dog Molly for a walk. Doris told her all about what was going on and how you started it all. So that's it, I'm afraid. But I am in a very good position to be of service to you. You see, I work as a political assistant to a Labour MP at Westminster. We know what's been going on here and are generally quite happy with what you have achieved, but I also have access to some information which is not very good.

"We got wind of a plot to destroy what you are doing. They are very powerful people. One is actually in the cabinet, and they have employed some MI5 renegades to cause you a lot of grief, starting with the murder of Doris and Molly. What your team did regarding those paedophiles was not appreciated in certain quarters and gave rise to this group, certainly implicated with that occupation, in order to suppress any news of that event.

"I have access to information through a friend in their service, an unhappy friend at that, who tells me what is going on. For example, they already know that you have taken the pawnbroker from Digby Circus. They don't know what you have done with him, but they suspect that you have killed him out of revenge. They say that he was of no importance, so as far as they're concerned, he was expendable. In other words, if you haven't killed him, he will be bumped off anyway."

"Hello, Reuben!" Amanita had heard the young man's voice. "How's Westminster these days now that the balance has gone back to the Eton boys and their minions? What a bunch! Gives new meaning to Hogmanay, what with pigs' heads and all that disgusting behaviour!"

Reuben was startled by the voice. "My god, Anna Rosita! What the hell are you doing here? We didn't know about you. We thought you were dead! How are you involved in this?"

"Oh, I'm just taking care of our pawnbroker friend, that's all. He just passed out. Might have been drinking too much, I think."

"You're not waterboarding the poor sod, are you?"

"No! We wouldn't do that, would we? Too damned expensive now that everything's metered!" Amanita turned to Sarah. "Sarah, love, could you take a look at him? He doesn't look too well to me. I'm no expert, but I'd say that he needs a little more than our tender care. Possibly a bed in a hospital ward would be a better option for the poor man."

Sarah left the lounge, a curious set to her face, but returned very quickly. "Poor old sod's had a stroke. We need to call him an ambulance at once. It's quite serious by the look of things. One thing's for sure—he won't be talking to anyone for a while. There won't be any sense to it."

Sarah looked long and hard at Reuben. He could sense that she didn't trust him.

"Sarah, I know my sudden appearance is not without certain problems. But quite seriously, you are very much in need of my services and my contacts. I understand what your aims are, and I'm fully engaged in that project. In my position, I can give you a great deal of information regarding the attitude of certain MPs. I believe this can be quite useful to you."

Everard had called for an ambulance to take the pawnbroker to hospital. He explained that he had found the man unconscious at the corner of the street and was unable to lift him.

Interrupting Reuben's assurances, Everard called out, "We need to get him down to the corner! There's an ambulance on its way, and I don't want them to have made a wasted journey. Quick, Sarah, take his arm ... Amanita, his left leg. You, Reuben, the other leg. We'll get him down there somehow, but there's not much time!"

It was done efficiently and quite quickly. They left the pawnbroker propped up against a wall, and the four waited out of sight for the ambulance to arrive. Sarah, however, continued to study Reuben. Everard seemed quite at ease, and Amanita obviously knew something that none of the others were privy to. So, as they returned to the flat, Sarah suggested that they should all eat out.

"I'll have to miss out on that this time. In fact, I don't need to be seen with you, any of you at any time, otherwise my ability to help you would be severely compromised. You do understand, don't you? In fact, I should really disappear right now. Look, here's my phone number and my address, but only use it when absolutely necessary, and be very, very guarded in what you have to say. I will contact you again in a few days." They all shook hands and then Reuben vanished.

"What do think, Everard?" Sarah inquired.

"Too soon to say. Why, what are your feelings?"

"Too soon to say!" Sarah replied "What do you know about him, Amanita? He seems to know you. And why did he call you Anna Rosita?"

"That's the pseudonym I used to get into the country as a refugee. I couldn't use my Roma name because it was a known fact that nobody in the British Immigration Department liked Roma people. Anyway, I've known him since I first arrived in London when he wanted to get me into bed and again later when I was in the army.

"He was what I would call thoroughly pissed off with the other officers. He was actually chucked out for insubordination. I haven't a clue why he joined up in the first place, which in itself is a bit suspicious. I think he needed to be in that position, but he definitely was not cut out to take orders. He was really out on a limb in the army. One has to be quite dedicated, and he wasn't. Maybe he had another agenda.

"I know he was arrested in the nineties for subversive left-wing activity, and that's how he got picked up by the Labour MP he now works for. I questioned if the assignment was bona fide or was he spying for Special Branch or MI6. He looks like he is on the level, but we need to take it day by day and keep a very shrewd eye on him. I must say, though, I don't like him, and he knows far too much about you two, that's for sure. So, definitely be on your guard just in case."

Sarah and Everard nodded in agreement. Amanita put her arm around Sarah's shoulder and said, "Good call earlier, Sarah. Shall we take you up on your suggestion and eat out? But sod the pizza. Let's have a decent meal with some proper wine. One thing though—having heard what Rueben said, I will be packing some insurance. Just keep your eyes open. We are obviously being watched."

Chapter 13

A couple of days had passed when Richie called by to reassure the trio that he and his parents were still safe and that his mum and dad felt secure. He spent the day with Sarah and Everard watching Amanita clean her various pieces of hardware before going down to the river to watch the Thames and blend in with the people. At around 6 p.m., Amanita suggested that they should snatch a quick meal at a pizza restaurant before taking Richie back to his folks.

An hour later, well stuffed with pasta and pizza, they left the restaurant. Amanita knew that Richie could easily be picked off if anyone knew anything about him. She was also aware that her presence with the young lad might attract attention, so she surreptitiously split from the others to keep an eagle eye on Richie and his surroundings as they navigated the streets to his family.

***

For some time now, Sarah had been thinking about her own situation. She had spent most of her adult life taking care of people. Never had she considered that she could become a target or that her life would be anything else than dedicated. But everything had now changed. Her attitude towards her patients had altered from one of caring to one of curiosity. She became more interested in what sort of people they were and their socio-political attitudes.

She started to assess what stance she should take when confronted by someone with right-wing views or somebody whose conversation turned to the importance of being wealthy. Or society's victims, some incapable of rising above the mire of poverty, some bereft of luck. Those she felt could be forgiven for some of their ingrained beliefs, but she knew of others who could not wait to get out of hospital to continue their assault on anybody that seemed vulnerable.

It was becoming a problem to her. She began to realise that she had started to become judgemental of those in her care because on their attitude towards others.

"Everard, I've been thinking. Since we've been together, I've realised that I am no longer the nurse that I used to be. It's not that I can't do the work but more a case of am I fit to do it. I've come to dislike intensely some of the people that I am meant to care for, and because of that, I think that I should put an end to it."

"Sarah, love, I've seen this happening to you for a while now. Just a few comments that you've made about some of those that you have taken a dislike to. It never happened before. But you're right. If you feel the way you do, it is obviously time to quit. Is there a chance of getting some kind of research post or something like that?"

"No. It's not what I want. You know, I look at Amanita, and I admire her. She has her problems as we all do, but she attacks them with such a positive attitude, almost uncaring of the consequences. That makes me think that I need to take some lessons from her.

"Honestly, Everard, I think our days are numbered. I don't like the way things have gone, and I'm seriously disturbed about Doris and Molly. If we are to die, I want revenge before it happens. We need to make our presence known and take as many of the enemy out as fast as we can. Where's Amanita? I think we all need to talk."

***

After Amanita had shadowed the group at a safe distance and finally saw Richie safely home, she took a detour back to the flat. It was really not surprising to see her one-time admirer lurking in the shadows with two others near Sarah and Everard's apartment. She swiftly vanished from sight into the blackness of the night, and using the colour of her clothing to her advantage, she took up a position in the hedged front garden of a house on the opposite side of the street.

She mulled over her options for a few seconds. Why were they there, and what were they about to do? But her mind soon focused as the three split up.

Reuben moved forward towards the door of the ground floor apartment. The other two moved to either side of the door at a distance of about ten metres. Amanita could see the glint of metal in their hands. Reuben looked from side to side to ascertain their positions and raised his arm to ring the doorbell.

Amanita raised her revolver and took careful aim at the back of his head. As Reuben fell, the other two broke cover. The first took two paces and the other four before they too stumbled and fell. *Dirty little snakes!* Amanita thought to herself. *More bloody work to shift these bastards. Everard and Sarah have to vacate this place pronto. I'm sure we'll work something out,* she reckoned.

Amanita rang the doorbell, took her key from her pocket, and entered, dragging the limp body of Reuben into the hallway behind her. "Everard, Sarah! Are you here?"

"Oh, no, Amanita! Not another bloody corpse!" Everard moved forward to help Amanita drag the body in and out of sight.

"Everard, call this number now! There are another two out there to be cleared up. This has now become a war which we could possibly lose. Take a look."

Pulling Reuben into the light, Amanita yanked his head up by the hair so that they could see precisely who she had killed. Everard blurted, "That bastard!"

Sarah exclaimed, "I knew it! I had a strange feeling about him the moment I set eyes on him. But I didn't think he'd show his colours so soon. What do we do now?"

Amanita searched through the other two conspirators' pockets and found nothing to identify them. Regardless, she was sure that they were members of the dark state's new secret police. They had been surreptitiously replacing the old Special Branch and were now using methods known to special security forces of other right-wing foreign powers.

Amanita remarked, "Look, we have to get out of here bloody quick. When no word gets back to their bosses, there'll be an all-out attack with the street being closed off and all our escape options sealed. So grab some stuff and let's leave these animals to the flies. I'm fed up with trying to clear away their mess!"

Sarah and Everard had never been too decisive, but Amanita's fears managed to penetrate and instil some urgency into the plan.

Everard looked to Sarah. "Sarah, have you got any money left?"

"Yes, I've still got about £4,000 in cash. What about you, Amanita?"

"Yes, don't worry. I've still got the contents of Hector's satchel. That man certainly had big pockets. Last time I looked there was about £9,000, and my only real expense since then has been my ammo."

"I've got another two and a half, "Everard said. "Altogether, we should be able to last a while as long as we keep out of sight. But what about when it's all gone?"

"We'll have to wait and see!" Amanita replied. Come, come! We should've been out of here by now. I've got Reuben's car keys. It's probably got a tracker on it, so we'll have to ditch it somewhere close to the MI5 building. That way it will give us a bit more time as they wait for Reuben to get back to his office. But we might gain an extra fifteen minutes, which will give us time to cross back over the river, get a cab each, and meet up at Victoria mainline. Okay?"

Everard had stuffed as much as he could into a small hold-all, not forgetting a framed photo of Doris and Molly. He stopped for a minute, and as Sarah re-joined him, he turned the frame to face her, and for that second, they stood silently to remember their memory.

"What about Richie?" Sarah asked Amanita. "If he calls here, they'll pick him up and probably his family."

"He won't come here tonight, but if we call him from a phone box at the station to warn him, he should stay safe. We can then make arrangements for all other possibilities when we can. Look, Sarah, this is still loaded. There are five still in the clip in case you need to fire it. Keep it in your pocket, and don't be afraid to use it. This one is for you, Everard. It's a bit heavy, so stick it in your belt and keep it out of sight. I have a stash of ammo which I can probably access tomorrow or the next day, depending on where we are. Let's go!"

The three slipped quietly out through the kitchen door at the back of the house and down the steps to the garden after locking the door behind them. They followed Amanita through the gate into an alley, at the end of which Amanita whispered, "Wait here!"

She slipped away into the shadows, and as she tried to start Reuben's BMW, she was surprised to hear a voice from the rear seat.

"Hello, Amanita. I wasn't expecting you!"

Amanita turned quickly, her gun pointed directly at the speaker's face. "Jesus Gerald! What the hell are you doing here?"

"I was actually waiting for Reuben. I owe him for a dirty little trick that he played on me. Slippery little bugger isn't he! What are *you* doing with him? I thought you and he fell out a long time ago. But then I'm often wrong when it comes to affairs of the heart."

"He's dead! I came for his car. He owes me too!"

"Well, well, well! So what are we going to do now? Are you still working for Hector? He's another one, you know. Don't like him — self-seeking, treacherous sort of man. Always has a strange odour about him as well. I could never place what it is."

"Probably shit! He's dead too! Look, I need to go now before the police arrive."

"No, I don't think I can do that at this point. You see, I know you and what you're capable of, and I also know that you've had dealings with a small cell that I've wanted to join for a long time. I don't like the way things have come about over the last few years, how we've all been sold out and lied to, and being on my own, I've discovered that I have no voice. So let's get away from here and go somewhere where we can have a sensible conversation."

Amanita found herself unable to break free from him and frankly found his ideology somewhat interesting. She quickly decided to acquiesce to his request without shedding more blood. "Right, but I have to stop off round the corner if you don't mind and pick up my luggage."

Amanita started the motor and slowly drove the car to where Everard and Sarah were waiting. Reaching the alley, she called out, "We've got company, you two! Quick, shove our bags in the boot. Everard, you in the back and Sarah beside me. Quick!"

Everard was not too pleased with the unexpected turn of events. "Amanita, lovely, but who the hell is this?" Amanita started the car, put it in gear, and drove away.

Without giving Amanita a chance to answer, Sarah blurted out, "I know you! I was your nurse in hospital about three years ago. You're Gerald Huntington, I believe."

"Yes, and I remember you too! A bullet deliberately found its way to my liver. I was the one with a very unsociable police guard throughout my unplanned stay. In fact, I was warned several times to keep my mouth shut or the next time I wouldn't survive. And do you know who put the bullet in me, Sarah?" Gerald asked.

"No, but I know there was a cover-up going on and you were the victim."

"Yes, and the gunman was Reuben Pratt. The bastard murdered my girlfriend right in front of me."

Driving within the legal limits so as not to attract attention, Amanita listened to Gerald's sordid account of his encounter with Reuben.

"I had loaned him some money some time before, and I thought it was about time he paid me back. It wasn't much, three hundred quid. So I arranged a meeting with him, and I thought Chloe, my girlfriend, would be an asset in the negotiations. When we all met up at his flat, he pulled a knife and cut her throat, then said to me, "Now how are you going to explain that … murdering my date in my flat with that knife?" as he threw it down in front of me.

"I wanted to slaughter the maggot, and as I bent down to pick up the knife, he shot me and left me for dead. His neighbours came down from the flat above, broke open the door, and got me to hospital. It was too late for Chloe, though. She was a lovely girl. I thought we might have … "

His voice cracked, and it took him a minute to compose himself and continue. Everard felt sorry for the man. "Take your time."

Gerald took a deep breath. "Anyway, it turned out that Reuben was with Special Branch or MI5 and was actually untouchable. The police put the pressure on me to keep quiet. And that's why I'm here. I'd been following that rat for weeks, and I thought that tonight I could put an end to him, but Amanita beat me to it.

"So you must be Everard and you, my dear nurse, are Sarah. I want to be part of the work you're doing. I don't know what part I can play, but I'm keen to do anything constructive.

"I knew Doris and Molly. We'd talk in the park sometimes, and she shared a lot about you, Everard, as if you were her son. She told me about the loan sharks and how you wanted to change things. I thought she was well on her way to do something about the state of affairs that we're all facing now, one way and another."

Everard was not certain about this newcomer but tried to cover his suspicions. "Doris was more of a moving force than I ever was. We're running away at the moment. That's hardly what one might call a driving force, is it?"

Gerald had an idea. "I don't think I'm on anybody's radar at present, so if you like, we can go to my place in Bermondsey unless you had plans to go somewhere specific. There's so much coming and going around there that nothing would look unusual."

Amanita nodded. "I'm okay with that. What about you two?"

Everard put his hand on Sarah's shoulder. "Agreed?"

"Yeah," came the quiet response.

Suddenly, "Shit! Shit! Shit! We've been spotted. There's a black Range Rover behind us, about fifty meters back. I'm going to try to lose him before I do anything drastic."

Amanita took a sharp left turn, and sure enough, the Range Rover was still following.

"There's a bar just down the road," she said. "I'm going to make out that we are just out for a drink. I'll pull over in a minute. We're going to need our hardware. Don't exit the car if they stop behind us. I'm going to leave the engine running and do a quick reverse, so hold tight and brace yourselves for a hefty crunch. And don't fire unless I say so."

The Range Rover pulled in a few meters behind them. Before the occupants got a chance to react, Amanita put the car in reverse and rammed into the front of the Range Rover. The boot of the BMW sprung open, giving some cover to the occupants at the back of the car. Immediately, she exited the car leaving everyone dazed and confused. Seconds later, she returned to her seat, slamming the car door closed.

"Damn it!" she burst out, pounding on the steering wheel. "I've never killed a woman before. This is so bad … so, so bad. My god, the look on her face as I sprayed the chlorine gas inside the car. I'll die still seeing her face."

Snapping out of her distraction, she urged, "Okay, everyone, grab the bags! There's a taxi over there behind the bar. If we can get to King's Cross, we can lose ourselves in the crowd. This way … away from the car. We'll get to the cab from the carpark around the back of the bar. Act tipsy and don't look worried. We're just two couples out for the evening."

The taxi driver, oblivious to what had just occurred, was happy to take the fare. At King's Cross, the two couples with arms around each other followed the lead of Gerald Huntingdon, who took them to a bus shelter not far from the station.

"We need to take the 188 to Bermondsey and get off at Bermondsey tube. It'll be a ten-minute walk from there. My god, Amanita, there's not much of you, is there. Just skin, bone and … Goodness! How many weapons have you got under there?"

"I'm alive because my small physique has enabled me to crawl into cracks in the wall if I need to, so don't knock it. Now put your arm around me and zip it!"

Everard and Sarah smiled. "Look, here's the bus!"

Gerald's flat was on the first floor of a squalid building in the centre of equally run-down row houses.

"Well, one thing's for sure, Gerald. You obviously live alone!"

Sarah picked up a cushion from the floor and moved aside a pile of clothes on the couch to make room for seating. Everard looked in the sink at the stack of used coffee mugs and then opened the loo door, which he quickly slammed shut.

Amanita had a look of devilment in her eyes as she asked Gerald what might be considered a difficult question. "Gerald, I don't wish to be too personal, but forgetting about the state in which you live, where on earth did you dream up your surname, Huntingdon? I mean, you're right in the heart of the British Isles, and you're definitely not totally English. So ... "

"Good question, Amanita, because it is exactly the same question I asked my parents. You obviously sussed out that I'm Jewish as were my parents. They had gone to Israel after they married and rented a small holding from a Palestinian family. They grew quite a lot of food, some of which was consumed by the local population, and everything was fine for about six years.

"Trouble came when some other Israelis wanted to build in what was still Palestinian-owned areas. The next thing my parents knew, their smallholding was being bulldozed. Olive trees were uprooted, and grazing turned into desert. When they protested, they were vilified as Arab troublemakers, and when they showed the marauders proof that they were Jewish, they were told that they should never pay rent for something that we, the Jews, already owned. It was too much for my parents, and they immigrated to the UK totally disillusioned. They changed their name from Goldberg to Huntingdon, basically to avoid any antisemitic persecution.

"To be honest, I have never broadcast my origins because as far as I'm concerned, I am British, just another person on this small island. What's more, I certainly don't have anything to do with religion in any way, and I don't go along with ethnic religion. That segregates society and causes prejudice. I suppose in reality I'm not one-hundred percent English. That should be reserved for those who have ancient roots here. But Huntingdon, although an old English name, works for me. What about you?"

Amanita smiled. "Gerald, I think we're going to get along just fine. My parents were Roma people from Kosovo. Their parents, my grandparents, had been gassed in Poland by the Nazis. Eventually my mother and father were rescued by a Russian brigade and taken to a hideout in Northern Albania.

After the war, they returned to their home where my father was murdered by Serbian soldiers at the beginning of the Balkan war. So you see, we have similar roots in an odd sort of way."

Everard and Sarah sat in silence. They had both heard and understood such stories but now it was so close to home that they found difficulty in confronting the reality of it.

Everard stood up trying to suppress what he felt. "Come on, let's have something to eat and a glass or two of wine before I start to eat your carpet, Gerald. And as for you, my dear Amanita, why didn't you tell us before? The two of you, both victims of your adopted country, don't seem to carry any hostility towards the people, only towards those involved in this new fascism.

"What I don't understand is that at one time we had so much support when Doris was in command, but I don't see it anymore. I don't know of anybody I could call on to help us if we needed to. Let's face it, none of us want control or power. All we want is a fairer society where people are respected and not abused.

"When I took Wragge's money, it was to pay all those who were his victims, but whoever is ruling now has just made things worse. It seems like those who were rescued from debt by Doris are back in the same situation, victims of a new generation of thieves who are likely supported by what must be a newly resurrected anti-social government. I seriously don't think that we can do anymore. Now we're on the run, and I don't like it."

Sarah looked sadly at Everard. "Is there nothing more that we can do? It seems like all those we knew now just pass us in the street and barely look up. We didn't even have the chance to bury Doris nor Molly.

"When I look back on those days when we were still fighting, everybody loved what Doris was doing. People even gave presents to Molly, but after their murders, the whole spirit of rebellion was gone. I think it's over, Everard. What do you think, Amanita? Is there any point in fighting on? Gerald, I think you have just come aboard a sinking ship."

Amanita was quiet and thoughtful while all four looked dismally into their glasses for some semblance of hope.

"We can still make a difference!" Amanita said excitedly. "We are now all outcasts. I know Gerald isn't on their radar as yet, but what if we made an attack on their centre of operations? Look, something that Hector taught me was that nearly all the right-wing male politicians have a subagenda, whether it's sexual or financial. If one can dig out some information on them, maybe … "

Gerald had other ideas. "No, it's going to take too much time, and we could end up going round in circles until they dig us out. Look, you all seem to have a bit of cash left. I have a good financial record and can probably raise at least another £10,000. So, publicity is the way. First of all, you will need a printer who is on our side. Then we publicise what they did to Doris and Molly. That will cause a real ruck! I have a friend at Channel 4 who I haven't seen for ages, so I could by chance meet up with him and mention the story and see if it gets picked up. It is big enough, and they do love to call on the government to account.

"Wait … I know I said find a printer. Forget it! Print your own pamphlets, get them delivered with the free papers or employ some out-of-work people who have an axe to grind. There's plenty of them on the streets. What do you think?" Gerald looked quite pleased with himself.

"That's brilliant, Gerald!" Sarah looked to be ready to go then and there. "I'll sneak down to the hospital tomorrow and see if I can find an ally to help this along. Patients are quite vulnerable to the news and, provided they're not hard-line fascists, most would be shocked by what happened to Doris and Molly. I don't know about you, Everard, but we were always in good spirits when they were around."

Everard put his arm around Sarah.

"None of this would have been possible without Molly. She played her part right at the very start and ultimately suffered the consequences. It's not right what they did. I would kill them over and over again if I had the opportunity."

Amanita chimed in, "Or get me to do it! Everard, you are definitely in need of some training if you want to hit a target, especially one that's moving."

Spirits were high and even Gerald, who felt a little left out when the subject of old times arose, made everyone feel much more at home. As the evening wore on, tiredness gradually took its toll, and he suggested that they should all retire.

"I don't know how to arrange this," he said, "but there is just one spare room besides my bedroom. Of course, there's the couch that you're sitting on."

Amanita spoke up. "Gerald, normally we three sleep together in one bed, but under the present circumstances, I think that Everard and Sarah can go in the spare room and I'll share your bed. I think you and I have some talking to do anyway. I feel I owe you an explanation for stealing your thunder, but I had no choice. Is that okay by you? I'd hate to put you under any pressure … though I could do with some myself."

This last comment was met by a stifled silence. Gerald looked pleased but surprised and not a little embarrassed. Sarah looked away, quietly snickering.

Only Everard appeared serious. He felt a little threatened. His relationship with Amanita complemented that with Sarah, and having had physical relations with both, he felt that he was being side-lined. At that moment, he lost a large part of his self-confidence. Sarah caught his expression and stopped giggling.

"Everard! You look like you've lost something!" Her tone was a little hostile, and she looked him straight in the eye. "I hope this doesn't mean that I've lost something too or, to put it in context, that I never had it to lose. So what is it?"

This was the first time that Everard had been questioned about his relationship with Amanita. He had always felt that he and Sarah, being brother and sister, were safe and that having

Amanita as a bedfellow was not so much as playing away from home as it was playing at home.

Gerald had no idea as to what was going on. Amanita, on the other hand, sniffed the air and suggested that she and Gerald should go out to get some more wine and telephone Richie to make sure he was safe. She practically dragged Gerald to the door,

"Won't be long!" Gerald called out. "Don't upset the neighbours with too much noise, will you?" and they were gone.

"What?" said Everard in response to the straight look that Sarah was giving him.

"What? Is that all you've got to say? Look Everard, I thought it was just us two. I never said a word against Amanita because she is really quite amazing and you were quite content to allow her into our bed. I never said a word because you seemed happy with the idea, and I was always a little terrified by our own relationship should anyone ever discover it. We might be brother and sister and cannot be parted because of that, but I also thought that your true feelings were for me and Amanita was just a temporary amusement. But it no longer seems that way and I'm not interested in becoming the third wheel. So if you're hankering after Amanita, then this is the time to tell me and be honest. If she wants to spread her wings, then that is up to her. Now tell me, what do you really want?"

Everard was in a state of shock. First Amanita and now Sarah had confronted him in a manner to which he was unaccustomed.

"Grief, Sarah! Suddenly everything has changed, and I'm having a problem sorting it in my mind. We've lost our home. We have a fourth member in our family. I feel that I am losing the love of someone I think very highly of, and I'm now in danger of losing you too. My ... *our*, relationship with Amanita has been very close, even as a friend, forgetting the bed stuff.

"But how much is the loss? If she gets really close to Gerald ... Well, we don't really know who he is or even if he's genuine.

What if he's actually an adept member of the enemy? If so, he already has Amanita, our bodyguard and good friend, in a very vulnerable position."

"That doesn't answer my question, Everard, and you know it. I'll say it again. What do you want?"

"It has to be you, Sarah! Of course, it's you. How could it be any other way?"

"That sounds a bit grudging. What if Amanita wants to return to our bed, what then?"

Everard was taken aback by her question. He looked at Sarah and faltered for a moment. The truth of the matter was that he loved both women for different reasons and wasn't really prepared to make a finite choice right then and there. Lamentably, Sarah saw that, turned her back and walked into the spare room, put her coat on and left the apartment.

"Goodbye, Everard. It was a pleasure while it lasted. When you want a sister, then I'll be available, but I think you have chosen your bedfellow."

Everard watched her from the window as she walked away. He wanted to call out to her, or to see her return, but the window was jammed. In the shadows cast by the dim streetlamps, Everard saw a movement and realised that Sarah was being followed. He grabbed the pistol that Amanita had given him, rushed down the stairway to the front door and out into the street.

It was almost too late. As Sarah turned the corner, Everard could see two figures grab hold of her and force her to the ground. A third figure jumped out in front of him as he raced towards Sarah. Everard rammed the barrel of the pistol into the man's forehead with such force that he heard the bone crack, and the assailant fell back unconscious.

Gaining on the others, he fired a shot, missing his target, but as one arose from his prey, Everard fired again. This time, the bullet found its mark, hitting the top corner of the man's pelvis, completely paralysing his target from any further activity. The third member of the group released his grip on Sarah, who lay motionless on the ground. He turned and took a shot at Everard before running as fast as he could out into the main street.

Everard thought he'd let him go, but another shot caused him to hesitate as he saw the figure stagger and fall. He could see a hypodermic syringe lying next to the silent body of Sarah and realised that she had been drugged, either to kill her or to knock her out. As he gently shook Sarah, he could feel a cool breath on his cheek and then the voice.

"We need to get away from here quickly, Everard. Gerald was a bit too forward, and so I gave him a push into the canal. Look, Sarah needs a doctor. Grab that syringe. We have to get back to Gerald's flat. Can you carry her? I need to find out who these characters are. I'll catch up with you later."

Amanita returned to the second of the three men who had eventually succumbed, quickly went through his pockets but found nothing of any significance except a single Albanian coin. A few people had gathered by this time.

"Is he all right?" one of the onlookers asked.

"No, he's dead, I'm afraid," Amanita responded. Could you call an ambulance? I think there are two more victims here somewhere. I heard several shots. Gangland stuff, I suppose. Is there much of it round here? Look, I have an appointment to keep. When the police arrive, give them this card. It's my husband's."

As the crowd grew in size, nobody noticed that Amanita had disappeared. She made a quick trip around the block and slipped back into the flat from a different direction.

When she reached Gerald's place, Everard was still trying to revive Sarah. "How is she? Is Sarah okay, Everard? Let me have a look. My god, we have to leave here as soon as she comes to. Give me that syringe, Everard. Get her bag and yours as well. I think I know what's going on here.

"Have you noticed that Gerald doesn't appear to own anything? There's no television, no radio or CDs or DVDs, nothing. There's enough food in the fridge for just one day. There are no other clothes in the wardrobe except an overcoat and only one roll of loo paper in the lavatory. For somebody who looked quite well dressed, he certainly doesn't seem to own much. I thought there was something funny going on. I think this is just a transition point for certain individuals.

"Thinking about it, it could be a Mossad setup looking to get Hector's list. I wonder if Hector was involved with them. He was rather two-faced when it comes to it. As I recall, there were names on that list of individuals who still have some power inside this new crowd in the government. A little bit of blackmail, and the ear of the prime minister could work wonders for Israel's desire to be rid of the Palestinians ... who knows?

"Look at this. I found it in the pocket of the guy you shot. It's an Albanian coin. I think Gerald thought he could hold Sarah and possibly me as ransom against that list. I wonder. As for you, I'm not sure what you would have been worth to them. You know, he had his hands all over me, but it was like he was looking for something other than my private parts. He might have thought I was wearing a wire, but he must have called those others up from Reuben's car. I'm wondering if he thought we were all part of Reuben's group. Anyway, when I chucked him into the river, he disappeared quite fast and I didn't see him come up again.

"Are you ready, Everard? I think Sarah's coming round. I hope so because we've got to leave right now." Amanita rose and walked to the window. "Come here, look out the window. What can you see?"

Everard peered through the grimy window. "There's a black limo just pulled up over the road. They're just sitting there watching what's going on. I think they must be part of Gerald's crew. What d'you suggest? They'll see us if we leave now. You're probably right. This is definitely beginning to smell like a Mossad set-up. It's too well organised for any amateur group. I think we've got to get out of here bloody quick!"

"Everard, they'll be up here in a minute or two. So plan A is for me to create a diversion so that you can get Sarah to safety. Or plan B, depending on how many are down there, we could ambush them here like we did at Doris's flat. Now that could get really messy ... Oh shit! They're already coming over! There are three of them and nobody else left in the car."

Within a few seconds, there was a tap at the door, and a low voice called softly, "Gerald?" The door handle slowly turned, and a tall, slim man holding a gun tip-toed in. Amanita brought all her attention to the head of the newcomer, whose vision was totally focused on the prostrate figure of Sarah on the floor in front of him. He stooped forward and fell without a sound. Amanita wiped the blood and grey matter from her stiletto on the man's shirt. She then closed the door very quietly once again and dragged the body into the bathroom.

Amanita whispered to Everard, "The other two will be up in a few minutes. Just keep out of sight unless I get into trouble, then use your gun. But I think it's best that we stay as quiet as possible. Hopefully, they will come in one by one. If they enter together, take this wine bottle and give number two a hard whack across his nose as he comes in."

There was a soft creak from the stairway, and Amanita braced herself for the second delivery. She wasn't expecting it to be as easy as the first especially since the smell of blood was beginning to permeate the room.

She decided to meet her opponent face to face. As the door began to open, she pulled it quickly towards her, and with as much force as she could muster, slammed it back into the body of the newcomer. It worked. He lost his balance, and stunned, the intruder lost his footing on the landing, taking himself and his accomplice through the balustrade, finally crashing one on top of the other at the bottom of the stairwell. Whether they were alive or dead, to Everard, Amanita and Sarah, it mattered not one jot.

Sarah had risen very unsteadily, made her way to what she thought was the bathroom, saw the ooze from the back of the dead man's head, and vomited over his back.

Amanita took Sarah by her arm and helped her down the stairs, to the street, and into the back of the black limo. Everard followed with their bags and anything else that might incriminate them in presumably a triple murder. Amanita had quickly taken the car keys, wallets and identification from all of her victims' pockets, and together they started to drive off.

As they reached the end of the street, a police car swerved across in front of them. A policeman jumped out and proceeded to approach them. He got within ten paces of the car but then unexpectedly stopped, stooped in a half bow, and waived them through, past the police car.

"What was all that about, Amanita? Did he recognise you or something?" Everard was genuinely puzzled.

"No! I didn't notice it before, but when I opened the boot for our bags, I saw the emblem near the number plate. We are driving in a vehicle with the CD plates of what seems to be the Romanian Embassy. What it does mean though is that we can't drive too far in it without attracting a lot of interest. I have a notion that they're probably fakes. It's the usual way of shifting blame if anything goes wrong, usually set up by nearly all of the spy networks, including our old friends in MI5 and Special Branch.

"This is all getting seriously complicated. I don't know if we're going to survive this! Our best bet is to rent a car after we dump this one outside the embassy. But what we'll have to do now is to get a hotel room for tonight and pick up something less conspicuous tomorrow. Sarah, how are you feeling? I'm sorry I couldn't do more for you, but everything was getting a bit too frantic."

Sarah was still very groggy. "I don't know what they put in me, but I feel very, very dizzy."

Amanita pulled over and Sarah leaned out of the window and vomited once again. Sarah wiped her lips and looked silently out the window.

"Sarah, would you like to go to hospital?" Everard asked.

"Oh, no Everard. I'm coming around a bit. It will soon pass, but thank you."

Everard shifted uncomfortably in his seat. He remained silent, deep in thought. It had seemed gratifying that Sarah had supported the inclusion of Amanita, but by doing so, he felt that their three-way relationship had become complicated. He had feelings for both women and now felt torn. Maybe the best thing was to end this triad, even at the risk of someone getting hurt.

"Sarah, Amanita, if we get a hotel for the night, I think it only right that we get two rooms, a double for you two and a single for me. I think there has to be a turning point in our relationships, and we need space to think this through."

Amanita turned towards Sarah. "It was bound to happen one day, I suppose. Today we're still alive, so let's just try to stay that way. It makes our mortal problems seem not as important as they were earlier. So, I agree with Everard. It will also give us the opportunity to find out how we get along without his presence."

Sarah turned and silently resumed looking out the window.

***

Having reached Palace Green, Amanita parked the limousine as close as she could to the embassy. Eventually, she found a space on Holland Street in a restricted area, and the three nonchalantly made off towards the Royal Garden Hotel.

Sarah muttered under her breath as they entered, "Can we really afford this? Can't we find something a little less ... "

"No!" whispered Amanita. "Nobody will be looking for us here, so we'll be safe for the time being. Everard, I suggest you book your own room, and Sarah and I will register ours. Hopefully, we'll all be fairly close to each other, but we shall see."

Everard completed his booking first, then sauntered over towards the lift and casually waited to be shown to his room. Sarah and Amanita, on the other hand, had a slight problem signing in owing to Amanita not having identity papers to prove her nationality.

"Madam, your accent is unmistakeably foreign, so I'm having a hard time believing you're a British national. You appear a little vague, and the photo in your driving licence shows a more corpulent visage than the one I am now looking at."

Amanita was outraged. "Who the hell do you think you are? That was taken five years ago, and since then, I have stopped eating as much, and yes, my grandparents were refugees and my parents arrived here long before you were born. Now get me the person who runs this place. I think your behaviour is insulting and unacceptable!"

"I'm very sorry, madam. Please forgive my intrusion into your privacy. Unfortunately, the government now stipulates that anybody who does not fit an altogether British type, for lack of a better word, must be thoroughly checked out. Please accept my abject apology."

The receptionist handed her a key to room 71. "A porter will lead you to your chamber. If you would like to go to the lift, there is one already awaiting you."

As they walked away, Sarah inquired "Whose photo is that in your driving licence? It's certainly not you, is it?"

"Oh, I don't know. I found it in one of Hector's coat pockets some time ago along with some blank passports and other blank documents. So I just made up a licence with that photo. I must say, I can't think what Hector had to do with that young woman, but I bet it was not in her best interests."

As they reached their room, Sarah spotted Everard peeping out from behind another door further along the corridor. She nodded in acknowledgement, and Everard withdrew from sight. Amanita and Sarah talked long into the night before falling asleep sideways across the bed.

Everard, on the other hand, lay silently examining his feelings, recalling the past errors and successes, all the deaths that had occurred since Wragge's demise. By six o'clock, he realised that the night had passed, and sleep was nothing more than a distant dream. He had noted Sarah and Amanita's room and stood by his door watching for any movement, an exercise that continued for nearly two hours. At eight o'clock, he knocked on their door. All was silent.

Damn! he thought. *At this rate, if they don't get up soon, we'll have to stay another night.* At that moment, Amanita opened the door just enough to peep out.

"Oh, it's you! Can't you sleep? What time is it anyway?"

"Eight o'clock. We need to get out of here before ten, otherwise we'll get charged for extras. Come on! Have a shower, get dressed, and where's Sarah?"

"I don't know! Isn't she with you?"

"No! Oh, grief … where's she gone? When did she go? Amanita, wake up!! We need to find her!"

Amanita started to laugh. "There you are! You see? You really do want *her*, don't you? She told me all about her worries with the three of us. So she now has her answer, and I shall no longer interfere."

At that moment, there was a cough from behind the door. Sarah peeped out with a wide smile across her face.

"That was a chance move, Amanita. But after last night, I think we all love each other enough not to want to change anything. We are three as much as we are one. Come in, Everard, and have some coffee with us while we get ready."

Chapter 14

At 10 a.m., Sarah and Amanita sauntered down to reception with Everard following at some distance. Amanita was chatting about nothing in particular, but as the receptionist approached and was within earshot, Amanita, in a slightly raised voice, declared, "When we get to Liverpool and have seen Jenkins, well take the ferry to Ireland and then take the ship to the states."

Sarah was a little bemused but took the bait. "It'll be good to see Jenkins again. He's always been a good friend."

The receptionist seemed not to listen, but after receiving the payment for the night, she bid them bon voyage with a smile.

Everard stifled a cough as he waited, and it was only when they were all out of sight of the hotel that they once again got together.

"Before we leave this area, there is something that I've wanted to do for years," said Amanita. "I want to visit the Serpentine Gallery across the gardens. I think that some of the gang I used to hang around with when I first arrived in the UK have some work on display. They were really kind to me when I was in my early twenties—you know, the good and bad times one has before life becomes serious. I'm not absolutely sure whether it will still be there, though. Are you up for it?"

Sarah was keen, but Everard was a little nervous.

"Amanita, it would be stupid to miss this opportunity, but I have some really bad vibes about today. When we left the hotel, I noticed that the receptionist used the telephone."

"Did you tip her, Everard?"

"Yeah, of course I did! Fifteen quid."

As the banter continued, Everard frequently checked to make sure that they weren't being followed. Within a few minutes, they had entered the foyer of the gallery, leaving their bags at the front desk.

Amanita studied the work on display and found one piece that she recognised. "Hey, you two! Look at this! That's me about ten years ago. It's by my then-best friend, Vanessa. I wonder how she got that in here."

Amanita stepped back a little and found herself gently held by another old acquaintance.

"Amanita! Well, what a surprise! I always wondered what had become of you. You still haven't put on any weight, though, have you? What are you doing these days, besides admiring your portrait?" The stranger laughed.

"Eric, get thee behind me! Have you given up on your bad ways or are you just looking for more victims to destroy?"

"Actually, my dear, I am working for Channel 4 investigating government misdeeds." Lowering his voice to a whisper, "Did you know you're being followed? When I spotted you, I noticed that there's a guy over there in a blue shirt who's been on your tail pretending to be looking at the paintings every time you look up. Where are your friends? I saw you with them when you left your gear at the desk, but they seem to have disappeared."

"Eric, quick, come with me. I need to find them!"

Amanita soon saw Everard sitting quietly outside the entrance to the female WC and let out a sigh of relief.

"Everard, thank goodness! Everard? Everard! Oh no!"

Everard didn't move. He had a fixed stare with his facial muscles completely taut. Amanita put her arm round him and found the end of a broken needle protruding from the back of his neck just below his skull. The collar of his shirt was rotting away into pale yellow fumes from the acid with which he had been injected.

"Shit! She exclaimed, near tears. With her adrenalin surging, Amanita rushed into the WC just in time to catch Sarah's last breaths. She was unconscious, her head having been smashed into the toilet bowl and her wrists slashed to the bone. Jarringly, her killer was still there, washing the blood from his hands and smiling to himself.

Amanita was in turmoil. She knew that her life was in danger, especially without her friends. Before the assassin could react, she flicked open her razor, and with all her strength, she thrust it hard and deep into the killer's belly, his flesh parting in a great gaping gash, heaving it upwards through his sternum and up into his throat. Her anger was so intense that there was nothing to stop her. Wiping the blood from her hands, she slipped the man's pistol from the back of his waistband.

"Typical! Bloody useless Webley. It'll have to do!"

Eric was still standing by Everard, trying to ascertain if there were any signs of life in the already greying corpse when Amanita reappeared.

"Eric, now, with me! Run! Run!" she screamed.

The two fled through the fire exit, hotly pursued by two more assailants. Amanita rammed the short barrel of the Webley into the first man's mouth and pulled the trigger, sending his shattered teeth flying out of his bloody cavity. Luck was with her for, as the bullet passed through the first man's neck, it propelled instantaneously into the forehead of the second.

Amanita quickly detoured back into the gallery entrance to snatch her bag from the desk despite a spirited defence from the security man at the door. Back outside again, she saw that Eric had been caught and was being dragged across the park to a waiting black Range Rover. Amanita took aim at the vehicle. It took two more shots to immobilise the car, both puncturing the nearside tyres. She then stooped down, unzipped her bag and took out her old faithful, a long-barrelled 9mm target pistol.

The man to the right of Eric fell immediately, but as the second tried to use Eric as a shield, he too fell, his leg buckling with his kneecap shot away. Eric ran towards Amanita but was caught in the arm with a bullet from the driver of the Range

Rover. Amanita paid him back in full, and the two fled from the park and finally managed to safely reach the Underground.

"Amanita! What the hell's going on? Who were they? Listen, I'm tracked by Special Branch at all times. Channel 4 has a habit of regularly upsetting the government. But this lot—guns, murder—what the hell are you into, Amanita? More importantly, what have you got *me* into?"

"You want a story, Eric? You've got one! Have you a safe house where we can talk? And make sure that you're transmitting what I tell you because what has happened is the culmination of a government using the most vile criminal elements to suppress any kind of dissent to the status quo! I'm serious about this. Is there somewhere safe that we can go to? A secure place where you haven't been followed?"

"The supermarket! There's a back exit to Tesco's that I found useful in the past to avoid certain people. It's near a squat where I've done a couple of interviews."

"If you think it's safe, then okay."

As they left the train, they split up but kept each other in sight while mixing with the crowd. Before long, they entered the portals of the supermarket. Eric passed through the stationery aisle, taking a packet of envelopes whilst Amanita chose an aerosol of penetrating oil. After the checkout, they disappeared into the gloom of dusk and the unlit entrance to Eric's safe squat.

Amanita flopped onto Eric's couch and stared wide-eyed at the opposing wall as if replaying the horrific events that had just transpired. The thin line between what was imaginary and what was real slowly evolved into the harsh truth ... Everard and Sarah were gone.

"Amanita, what's happening? Are you okay?"

Her face in her hands, she cried inconsolably—for Doris, for Sarah, for the only man she had ever loved.

Eric sat beside her, his arm around her shoulders. "I know, Amanita. I'm so sorry. It wasn't supposed to be this way.

But it's important that we get on with fighting for the cause they gave their lives to. They need you to carry on for them, for those who have suffered for far too long. Can you do it, Amanita?"

She nodded, wiping away her tears, vengeance and hatred searing her life force.

Eric took out his phone. "Are you ready, Amanita? We can't stay here too long, otherwise the signal will be picked up. I reckon we've got about three quarters of an hour before they start looking for us. Off you go. This is going directly to our programming unit."

In a monotone voice, Amanita recounted the entire story from the beginning. She tried not to leave anything out and included a confession to all the killings in which she had been involved.

Eric was horrified by the sordid series of events but realised that the information that he now held was sufficient to bring a very hostile response to the government's interminable incursions into public liberty. He knew that should the story be broadcast, the government would fall and that the deeply secret assassination squad would disappear underground. Any new regime would need to hunt the agents down and destroy them. That would never be an easy task.

Having sent the interview straight to his office, it was now down to the broadcaster to take action. The first thing was a leak of the interview to the left-wing press. The programmers checked and double-checked many of the details in the interview. Despite the government's botched attempts to conceal the truth, the interview was deemed to be genuine.

It was decided not to advertise the programme in the normal way. Instead, the channel gave it the title of "A Programme of National Importance" and gave no clue as to the contents. It was also agreed that Amanita's anonymity was to be respected, and all those involved in the production would not divulge confidential information regarding any of the players. Finally, it was decided to broadcast the item from outside the UK, knowing fully that the government would attempt to sabotage the system as soon as they became aware of the contents.

The broadcast lasted an hour at peak viewing time, and within fifteen minutes, Channel 4's switchboard was jammed by people wanting to add their experience of what Doris, Everard, Sarah, and Amanita had achieved and how their lives had been changed for the better. But one voice stood out over all the others.

Richie's call was broadcast after the programme. What he had to say was enough. As a witness, he was immediately surrounded by a wall of security. His family was kept safe by large groups of the populace. No security agent of the government could silence him without causing a massacre.

The government collapsed. All those in Westminster who were seen to be on the right of the political spectrum were rounded up and examined. Those found guilty of either working with or supplying data to those operating in the dark side of so-called security were imprisoned for either sedition or accessory to murder. What was never explained was how such a corrupt government could have crept back into power unseen and how they had taken over the reins of government and commissioned such heinous activity. It was almost as if they had never left despite the utopian revolution.

Amanita realised that she no longer had the support that she once had, but she and Richie had one last thing to do to remind the world that things could have been better. They raised sufficient money to commission a monument to Doris, Everard, and Sarah in bronze pictured with the ever-faithful Molly at their feet. It was a reminder of the price that was paid in order to cleanse the state of the evil that money exerted over those in power.

A new all-party government was formed. It sought conversation with all sectors of the public including the homeless and drew up plans to ease the burden on the poorest in society. The purge of loan sharks continued as did the closing of many sections of the gambling industry to ensure that it became more difficult for those with a propensity to that addiction to find themselves with serious financial and social setbacks.

Faith schools were no longer funded by the state but still inspected by an increasingly thorough commission. God was no longer on the agenda of the public purse, and private schools had to become self-sufficient or close. New state schools were built with the money saved, and universities and colleges were no longer able to leave places open for the old elite. The health service was healed after the abolition of the Public Finance Initiative, and the increase in available funds allowed an increase in staff wages.

Recruitment of a larger work force became easier now that there had been an amelioration of the attitude towards the once hated European Union. The future was beginning to look bright.

***

Nonetheless, Amanita was still nervous. She had thrown aside any idea of rebellion but felt anxious for Richie's well-being. As he grew, they spent almost every day together, with Amanita teaching him how to use the weapons that she had now decided to give up. Richie chose one gun only, Amanita's favourite 9mm target pistol. He had no idea that the time would come that he might have need of it. Richie was now sixteen and still living with his parents. His mother noticed that as the days passed, he was becoming more thoughtful.

"Richie, luv, you've got something on your mind, haven't you? I think I know what it is, and you should know that we are not going to stand in your way."

"I didn't want to say it because I didn't know how you would react. I want to stay with Amanita. Is that what you thought?" Richie slowly looked up at his mother.

"Yes, that's what I thought. You can't hide these things from your mum, can you? Have you spoken to her about it? You don't want to put yourself upon her if she doesn't want you to be there."

Richie felt a little relief that his mother was so understanding after all the trauma that had trailed them all since Everard and Sarah came into their lives.

"Yep! We've talked about it a lot, but she said that I must speak to you rather than just leave without a word. So, are you okay with me going?"

Lyn wiped a tear from her eye whilst pretending that the washing up was the most important thing in her life.

"Yes, luv! Your Dad and I have spoken about it, so it's not a surprise, and I think now that Amanita has given up killing people, you will be quite safe in her company." They both laughed, the one more genuinely than the other.

"Dad will help you take your stuff over to her place, but remember, if you need us at all, we are always here."

At the end of the week, Richie took up residence with Amanita who welcomed him with a warm hug.

"Richie, I am so happy to see you here. It's almost like having my own family. I never realised how lonely I had become now that all of our friends are gone." Amanita's words faltered as she recalled all that had happened and the precious lives lost.

Chapter 15

Richie and Amanita settled down in a closely knit mother-son bond. Richie adored her, and she in turn paid as much attention to him as was possible without disturbing their filial closeness, difficult as that may have been at times. Amanita was no less attractive than when she first made contact with Everard and Sarah and so, with Richie growing into manhood, she felt it necessary to maintain boundaries.

Amanita occupied herself as an agency care worker, avoiding situations where her past might be unearthed.

Richie was working in the local department of Parks and Gardens. He had taken Everard's advice and quit smoking. No longer was he the scrawny little dark-eyed lad in the playground but had grown to a healthy five-feet-eleven young man with a crop of unruly dark hair. Because of his deep outdoor complexion, he and Amanita did, to all intents and purposes, appear to be mother and son. She considered that when she and Richie saved enough money, they would go back to her village in Bosnia to seek out whoever remained of her relatives and introduce Richie to them and her past.

Amanita had developed the desire to discover during her free days more of the history of the country that had taken her in, especially the period after the Balkan Wars. Catching a train to Rochester in Kent, she then took a bus to Rochester Castle and the cathedral. It was a quiet time of year. Schools' half-term holiday had passed as had Guy Fawkes night, and with the days shortening, tourists were few and far between.

She took a room in a lovely Victorian hotel on High Street, paying for a week in advance.

The next day on a bus to the centre of the town, she had the misfortune of sitting next to a fifty-odd-year-old male with an unfortunate odour of beer and cigarettes.

"Hello, lovey! Got enough room here for you." He shuffled up to make a little more space for her. Amanita would rather have sat elsewhere but the lack of seats precluded that.

"Yes, thank you," she replied without looking at the geezer.

"You're a good-looking bird, ain't cha? I bet you've got a nice pair of tits under that coat. 'Ere do you want to touch this?"

He peeled open his overcoat and produced what had the appearance of a dried-up vegetable. Red to the extreme with a peculiarly scabby foreskin. He grasped her hand to force her to touch the abhorrent appendage. Amanita rose abruptly and glared with intense hatred at the miserable scumbag. She knew she could destroy him with one hand but chose to turn her back instead. The abuser persisted.

"Lovely legs, and look at your butt. Cor! I could give you one, that's for sure!"

Amanita turned and smacked him with a force that almost made the bus rock. She looked around at the other passengers and could sense their hostility. One man got up from his seat and confronted her.

"You're a fuckin' foreigner, you witch! You're a dirty Roma, ain't cher. Don't think I don't know your sort. I've been there, Bosnia, looking after your lot. I know what you are! You're a dirty gypsy witch, just like the rest of your Roma shits! Look what yer've done to 'im. Fuckin' dead, ain't he! You fuckin' killed 'im!"

Indeed she had. The force of her blow to his face had broken his neck against the rail at the back of the seat, his overcoat still wide open showing the withered item lying limp by his inert right hand. The bus driver stopped the bus and stood up to get out of his cab.

"Cover 'im up, he ain't decent. Poor man!" he ordered as several of the other passengers moved forward to corner Amanita. She didn't resist as they closed in on her, being certain in her own mind that justice would follow her to the court where it would be seen as justified to have hit the disgusting creature in the way that she did.

The body of the man was carried off the bus and propped up on a nearby bench as if he were watching the traffic going by. But Amanita was taken in the centre of a crowd to a nearby public house and cast into a dark room at the back of the cellar.

She was visited regularly by her accuser and his associates, all from a far-right group made up of riffraff whose hatred of women had already been marked by a rise in the quantity of rapes in that area over the previous years. They had drugged Amanita, then bound and gagged her and left her to the base and carnal inclinations of her eight jailers.

When she came to, she found that her clothes had been removed and that now all she had was a plain white cotton shift fit only for one sole purpose. After that, she was left with no food or water for days while plans were made for her departure.

When the door was finally reopened, Amanita was almost beyond reach from dehydration and lack of food, unable to stand after the ropes across her calves and wrists had been removed.

"Shit! We'll 'av to carry the filthy slag out. Bill, you've still got yer work clothes on. You can carry her. She probably don't weigh no more than a bag of crap. Just wash yer hands after you get her into the cart, then we'll wheel her up into the lorry."

***

Richie had been searching for Amanita for days without luck. Nobody had seen her, which struck him as odd. He knew she was somewhere in Rochester and would have been seen by somebody, but there was nothing.

Sixteen days had passed since Amanita had disappeared, and as Richie stood in a bus shelter wondering what to do next, he saw a poster promoting an event arranged by a historical re-enactment society. It proclaimed *The Burning of a 17th Century Gipsy Witch* at Leeds Castle on November 29. Richie thought that this was much too coincidental and decided to attend, realising that this might involve Amanita. If true, then she was probably in danger. It was worth the chance.

Packing his now favourite pistol and thirty rounds of ammunition in his belt, he drove his old car to the event. The crowd was huge, swarming like flies around a slaughterhouse. Richie noted the security, which was unusual. The ticket sellers were guarded by a crew of heavyweights who scanned the crowd for anybody that they deemed to be suspicious.

He saw an old wheelbarrow leaning against a tree some distance away, it's driver asleep close by, still clasping a half-eaten sandwich in his left hand and the remains of a spilled can of lager in the other. Richie thought this was probably his only chance to get in without the heavies suspecting him. The gardener's coat was at hand, and without a sound, Richie claimed the workman's persona, filled the barrow with dead leaves under which he hid his weaponry, and proceeded to the gate.

"You can't come in here without a ticket!" demanded one of the heavies.

"What do you mean! I bloody well work here. I don't need a ticket to get on with my job. Come on! Get out of my way!" and he passed the guard without being suspected.

He pushed the barrow around the perimeter of the event and was horrified to see what was happening. Secreting himself within a dense rhododendron bush, he loaded his pistol and watched. Vendors were selling rotten tomatoes and soft fruit to throw at the witch as she was led past on a tumbril.

Amanita was almost unconscious, the white shift splattered with mouldy fruit and stained with blood and urine. She was as pale as death, the tightness of her bonds constricting the blood flow to her hands and feet. Her voice had disappeared, from a beguiling Bosnian accent to a mere croak. Her hair was stuck across her face from the filth which her captors had thrown at her.

Richie was devastated and began to understand that his options to save her were closed. He knew she was about to die. All he could do would be to change the way in which that might happen.

Amanita had become delirious and started to laugh at the crowd as she was being hoisted onto the pyre. Old wooden pallets, fallen branches, and broken furniture made up the heap. Her shift had been ripped open, her breasts bare for all to see, black with the bruising and beatings that had been her punishment for being a Roma woman.

It was at that moment that Amanita came to and saw her fate clearly. She screamed with all that she had left. "Murderers! Murderers!"

The crowd loved it. This was reality, a re-enactment of a heretic's punishment some 350 years before. They cheered and clapped and chanted "Burn her! Burn her!" over and over again. Ignorance and apathy had blinded them from the truth, and crusaders for justice had become the enemy. *How did we come to this?* thought Richie.

It was then that Amanita saw it. Sunlight glinting in the distance on a small piece of metal. Having had enough, she screamed with what was to be her last breath, "Do it! For god's sake, do it!"

Richie could not hear her over the noise of the crowd but could see her pleading to him, her eyes fixed in his direction. Richie understood. Barely a second passed before Amanita's head fell forward against her chest, a small trickle of blood flowing down from her brow onto her shift.

The executioner, her accuser on the bus, stepped forward, and as he put flame to the pyre, he tripped and fell forward. As the flames leaped up, pieces alight tumbled down, and within seconds, he too was consumed. The crowd cheered even louder, drowning out his dying screams.

Richie could do no more, his tears clouding his vision to such an extent that aiming and firing again became impossible. He took the opportunity to leave whilst the attention of the crowd was focused solely on the incineration of Amanita and her would-be executioner.

The gate had become unmanned as the heavies joined the festivities, giving Richie the opportunity to leave without being noticed. The gardener was still sleeping as he replaced the wheelbarrow just as he had found it, tucked the pistol back into his belt and left, leaving no trace of his presence whatsoever. His mind rolled over and over the murder of his mentor, his dearest friend, his mother figure, and above all, the great love in his life. Nearly all was gone except the memory of her, and the faces of those involved in her death, his dearest Amanita.

***

Having returned to their empty flat, Richie was in total despair. All he could think of was vengeance upon those who he held responsible for the death of Amanita. After a couple of days, he called his employer to say he needed some time off and headed back to Rochester. He found a bed and breakfast accommodation for the following week and commenced his search for Amanita's captors. He had more or less emptied Amanita's armoury and was ready as ever to act.

Nobody knew anything, or so it seemed, but on the third morning, the owner of the B&B handed Richie the local newspaper. It struck Richie that there was no mention of the previous week's happening at Leeds Castle, but turning to the obituary notices, he saw the first chance to claim his revenge.

In Memory of Archie Lumpkiss, sadly missed by his friends and comrades, claimed by our Lord at Leeds Castle 29th of November on the occasion of a historical re-enactment. Memorial service to be held 5ᵗʰ of December at 10:00 a.m., Swindler Funeral Home

Richie realised that up to that point in time, his contribution to the event had not been noticed, which meant that he was unlikely to attract any attention if he attended the memorial. Not only that, he recalled Amanita's first appearance with Hector dressed all in black, and he felt that the example would not only be a tribute in a minor way to her but would also give him good cover on the night of what he hoped would be a fitting end to the escapades of those he had grown to hate.

A cold north wind was blowing all that day, and only a few people attended the memorial, but sure enough, there were seven faces that Richie recognised from the Leeds Castle killing. He made sure to keep far enough away so as not to attract any interest but followed the group as they made their way to the public house in which Amanita had been held.

He had armed himself to the teeth with Amanita's weapons concealed around his body—a pistol under his left arm, a fitted silencer, her stiletto neatly secure around his waist, and her razor in his trouser pocket. His immediate choice would always be the stiletto first and the pistol second. The razor he was unsure about, it being particularly messy and the problem of explaining the presence of so much blood on his clothes at the B&B.

When he entered the public house, he noticed that one of the group was in fact the publican. This pot-bellied individual leaning forward from behind the bar, whose thin hair stuck reluctantly to his greasy brow, struck Richie as the person most likely to have abused Amanita the most. As such, he would need more attention than the others.

The huddle drank enough to start reminiscing about their achievements, of the women they had taken, abused, and murdered. They had no idea that Richie's hearing was better at catching their words than their tongues and eyes were at keeping their guard.

"God, if we had known the trouble that fuckin' gypsy would cause, we would 'av got rid of 'er the first bleedin' evening, no doubt about that! But 'e wouldn't 'av it, would 'e. Nah! Wanted to play with 'er, 'e did, silly idiot! D'yer remember that when 'e screwed her the second time, he came out white as a sheet, never said a word, but she had scared him, that was for sure and then 'e said, 'Go on, you lot! Get in there and do 'er, the lot of you! Make sure you 'urt 'er as well.'"

Richie's hand grew ever tighter on the glass of red wine that he had been slowly consuming, but there was more to come. The publican had not finished his recital.

"D'yer know, when I got on top of 'er, I whacked 'er one with my fist right in 'er eye. Yer know, she never blinked, not once, just looked up at me, and then I got this pain right up inside me so I got off, kicked 'er in the crutch and left her."

Another one of the crew wanted to share his experiences. "It was that scar on 'er face! That put me right off. That was a wound and a 'af. That's a fighting scar not a bloody accidental one. When I saw that, I knew she was trouble! Not like that little Polish tart. When I started to do her, she started crying for her mum, so I told 'er if yer mum was 'ere I'd do 'er too! With that, the bitch bit the end of my nose, so I slugged 'er with 'af a brick. That taught 'er a bleedin' lesson, didn't it! She's the one that started to float after we chucked her in the Medway. Bloody good thing that barge bashed into 'er, 'cos that was the last time she'd ever 'av the chance to float!"

Each one of that group was keen to add his experience with either Amanita or some other poor girl or woman that had the great misfortune of falling into their hands. Richie sat almost in a trance, trying desperately to keep his hand away from his gun. All other customers had left the pub, and only he and the gang remained.

Finishing the last drips from his glass, he bid them farewell and disappeared into the darkness. Looking carefully around while he loosened the zip of his jacket, and making sure that nobody could see him, he slipped behind the public house into the car park, retrieved a short length of scaffold piping laying on the ground, and placed it strategically against the pub wall. He then retired into the shadows and waited.

The first of the group left alone and staggered to the rear of the public house not far from where Richie was waiting. He opened his zip and proceeded to urinate against the pub wall. Richie was as silent as a cat on the prowl. He stealthily approached his victim, and with a swift upward thrust, the man fell with no more than a grunt. Richie wiped the blood from the stiletto on the victim's coat and returned to his hiding place.

Not long after, two more arrived, and tripping over the corpse of the first, they turned their heads to face the killer. It was too late. Richie smashed the two heads with the metal bar in one stroke, breaking their jaws asunder, their spewed teeth rattling onto the tarmac like falling raindrops. Richie checked that both were dead and once again retreated to his hiding place in the deepest shadows.

The fourth was more problematic. He stood for a while silhouetted by the streetlamp which spread light across the front of the pub. The distance was too great for Richie to catch the man off guard, so he wrapped his scarf around the pistol, tightened the silencer, and fired. The noise was just enough to make a dog bark in the distance followed by dead silence. Richie pulled the man out of the light and dragged the body to the heap that soundlessly proclaimed the night's gruesome activity.

The next two followed the fourth in the same manner, leaving but one, the landlord, to deal with. Richie was beginning to feel weary having never killed anyone before. His muscles ached from dragging the corpses around. Remembering how Amanita had delivered the bodies to the railings at Westminster, he began to realise just how strong she must have been.

He took a deep breath and tried to concentrate on the last one, the publican. Richie made his way towards the door of the bar, which was still slightly ajar. He withdrew to the corner of the building to wait.

It was taking a while, about forty minutes already gone, and Richie was becoming impatient. The waiting paid off. The man exited the pub and started to bolt the door.

"Quick, quick!" Richie called out. "I think somebody's fallen down your cellar steps! Quick! They're calling for help but I can't see anything! It's too dark!"

The publican grabbed a torch and rushed out. "Where? Show me!"

Richie was pleased. It was working. "Hurry, they're round here!"

Richie sidestepped the pile of bodies, but the frantic publican, unaware of the obstacle, tripped and fell face down over them and onto the gravel. Richie placed his foot on the man's neck and leaned forward to exert as much pressure as he could.

"What the hell!" the publican croaked as he tried to raise himself against the pressure on his neck.

Richie slipped the stiletto out from his belt and sank it to a shallow depth around the victim's shoulders, back. and buttocks. As he did so, he made sure to exert enough weight on the man's neck to stifle any screams. The publican was desperate, and with a mighty heave, he rose a foot from the ground only to find the blade firmly angled against the top of his spine, ready to slip upwards into his brain.

He slowly went down again and whispered to Richie, "What do you want? Is it money? What!"

"Do you not see what you tripped over, you bastard?"

"Oh, god! You've killed them all! Why ... why ... why 'av you done this?"

"You and your friends there killed my mother. You brutalised her in the worst way, then you burned her. And you're asking me why I've done this, you piece of shit?"

Richie was trying to think what Amanita would have done under those circumstances. The man had to die, that was for sure. He had tortured her and been party to the murder of other women too. But then he knew Amanita was always so sure of what needed to be done. *The man needs to die so kill him. Don't mess around, Richie!* Her voice was in his head, clear and imperative.

Leaning over slightly without losing his hold, Richie grabbed the piece of scaffolding and placed it across the back of the publican's neck. Then with his right foot on one end, he stomped with considerable force upon the other and heard the terrible crunch as the last ray of light dimmed and faded from the man's eyes. No dogs barked. There was no noise, nothing to give away the death sentence he had just carried out.

The lights in the bar had been left on, so Richie slipped inside the pub to turn them off in case they attracted any attention. Just outside the pub, he saw a blackboard with the day's special nailed against the outer wall. A stick of chalk was on the narrow ledge of the frame. As a parting gesture, Richie wrote:

Free Food and Drinks Today
Help Yourselves
Plenty More in the Cellar

Richie slipped away knowing that by the time the police discovered the bodies, the crime scene would be too compromised to find any clues to the killer's identity. He removed his Mac, unzipped the inner lining, put the lining on, and discarded the bloodied raincoat in a secluded bin.

Tracing his way back towards the B&B through alleyways and unlit streets, he finally reached his destination around three in the morning. To allay any suspicions should he be seen, he took on the persona of an inebriate, the perfect cover at that ungodly hour. Besides, no drunk could possibly kill so many strong men in such a short space of time. He spotted an empty bottle of rum at the base of a lamppost, and staggering, he made his presence known to several of the CCTV cameras dotting the streets.

Breakfast at the B&B was usually served between 7.00 and 8.30 a.m. Richie had noted that there were two doors to the dining room, one near the stairs to the clients' rooms and the other near the front entrance. He had also noticed that the telephone was close to the bottom of the stairs.

Up to that point, he had spent the latter part of the night in his car in the rear carpark. Having secreted his weapons within the vehicle, he retrieved his mobile phone from under the driving seat and proceeded to the door of his host, keeping out of sight from any overlooking windows. Once there, he called the B&B.

"Good morning, Mr. Morgan. It's Richard Erskin in room four. What is on the menu for breakfast this morning?" Keeping the attention of the landlord for a couple of minutes, Richie sneaked into the dining room unseen, removed the raincoat liner and placed it on the seat next to him. Quickly, he sat at a table with the morning paper until Mr. Morgan discovered him.

"Oh, Mr. Erskin! I didn't realise that you had come down. Sleep well?"

"Yes, thank you. Visiting all these historical sites is quite exhausting. I haven't slept that well for ages. I shall be leaving you this morning round about nine to nine-thirty. I shall definitely be recommending this place to my colleagues!"

The proprietor smiled. "Why, thank you, Mr. Erskin! It's much appreciated. Now what can I get you for breakfast this morning?"

By 9.15 a.m., Richie was gone.

***

The police had been called to the public house, and as Richie drove past, he noticed a large crowd of early drinkers clutching an assortment of liquor bottles and packets of crisps. The police were trying desperately and with great difficulty to keep the group away from the crime scene. Others were engaged in photographing the corpses and searching for any forensic material.

Richie laughed for the first time since Amanita's death. "Mass Gangland Killing in Rochester" was the headline in most of the following day's newspapers. It was only later, after an examination of the cellar and the discovery of DNA from various women reported missing, that the police decided to change their lines of enquiry and seek out any other members of the publican's crew who may have been involved in the abductions of those women.

Chapter 16

Having finished the work of eliminating those guilty of causing the death of Amanita, Richie decided to leave the country and make his way to Bosnia. He was desperate to look for any of his adoptive mother's remaining family. It was only right to return Amanita's weapons to her relatives should they too find themselves subjected to another fascist scourge. Secreting them in various sections of the soundproofing felt under his car's bonnet, Richie took the ferry from Portsmouth to Caen in Normandy. Once in France, he was free to continue without any hindrance through northern Italy and eventually into Bosnia. It was for him the beginning of a new adventure into a world beyond the boundaries of London.

Having lived with Amanita for several years, they had accrued many possessions, and in the days following her death, he had managed to gather up all her things that he could find in their flat. Her clothes were a problem to him. They represented in his mind the last images of their shared life together, and he could not bear to dispose of them. Eventually, everything, clothes included, were carefully packed away and lodged at a storage depot for delivery when he felt safe enough to settle down once again. Money had been saved from one job to another by both of them, and during his journey, he had little problem with his accommodations and basic needs.

Amanita had told him all about her life in Bosnia, how badly the war had affected her Roma people. With that information, he knew more or less where to start his search for any of her relatives. Amanita had taught him the basics of her language, and though he had trouble avoiding his East End slant on the pronunciation, he seemed to manage quite well once he had arrived in Bosnia.

His first call in northern Italy was at Bolzano, and within a few days, he reached Potocari where he was directed into Skelani. There, a young woman about the same age as Richie was the first person he met as he parked his car on the roadside.

"Excuse me, Miss!" he called as she scuttled away, frightened. "Excuse me! Do you speak English?"

"Yes, a little," she replied, keeping her distance.

"I am looking for the family of Sanela, also known as Amanita. Amanita Virosa."

She stopped short and turned to face him, her head turned to one side.

"How do you know her? Where is she? She is my aunt." The young woman turned back to meet Richie face to face. He could see Amanita there in her eyes, her lips, and the way her hair tumbled down the sides of her face. It was a young Amanita who stood before him, the same slight menace in her expression. Richie was very nearly speechless.

"My name is Richie, and for several years, Sanela and I lived together. She was like a mother to me. I come from England with very bad news, I'm afraid."

The young woman grabbed his jacket lapels in a very threatening manner.

"What has happened to her? What!"

Richie stuttered, "She has been murdered, and I have come to return her possessions to her family."

She slowly released her grip. Richie could see the distress in the young woman's eyes as tears flowed down her cheeks and her voice lamented Amanita's death.

Richie questioned her, "Did you know her well?"

It was a pathetic response to the woman's grief, but it was all he could think to say, and he too found that his tears could no longer be held back. She hung on to him as her knees weakened.

They held each other as if their grief made them no longer strangers.

The young woman looked up at Richie. "I am Mirela and my father is Sanela's uncle. He was lucky to have survived the war, not like his sister, Hafiza. Those monsters! Come with me. Bring your things. I will take you to my father."

Richie was not a little confused. He had spent several weeks searching for Amanita's family, and suddenly, there they were, all that remained of them, welcoming him into their home. Rugged, weatherworn, and with a four-day stubble holding his face together sat Amanita's uncle.

"Sit down, young man," he said in a thick Roma accent. "Sit down beside me. Would you take tea with us?"

Richie nodded as he fumbled in his pocket for a small box.

"Sir, I am very sorry to say that Amanita, I mean Sanela, has been murdered in England. I have dealt with it as Sanela would have wished, and her killers no longer exist. She has been like a mother to me. We lived together and she taught me everything that I needed to know in order to survive. Among her possessions, I found a small box with something in it that I think you should have."

He handed the box to his host who opened it with a kind of passive excitement.

"My sister's blood! Sanela said that she would keep it safe and that it would come back to Bosnia if anything happened to her. She has kept her word. Tell me what happened to her, if you can, and call her by the name that she carried in your country. Amanita is what others here call her as well but we know her only as Sanela."

Richie told them the whole story from the very beginning to the end, including the final outcome.

"So, it was you who killed her! It is a brave person to kill somebody who one cares for, but as you have described, she had a less painful death than if she had been burned alive. What sort of people live in your country now? We used to dream of escaping to Britain because it was safe, but after what you have told us, we would not be welcome. You must be tired from your search and hungry, so we will have supper and we will find space for you to sleep."

Richie was not expecting such a hospitable invitation and thanked the gentleman profusely. They chatted until nightfall with Richie answering their myriad of questions about Amanita's journey and experiences since leaving Skelani.

The next morning, Richie found himself lying next to Mirela on a soft rug in a corner of the main room.

She smiled as he awakened. "I hope you slept well. You see we don't have a lot of space, two rooms only and no beds. I am afraid that this is how we have to live now because we have to be ready to move in an instant if there is any trouble coming. That is how we have survived. Those who didn't run are no longer with us and also that is why we were so hard for you to find. Do you have soap? If you do, we can get water!"

Richie was surprised. He had barely woken and was already told a story that he knew nothing about. He pondered for a moment.

"Have you got a shower?"

"Only if it is raining," came Mirela's quick response.

***

It seemed curious to Richie that within their own territory, their own home, these Roma people were isolated, out of touch with the outside world and only able to survive within their own sphere. To Mirela, Richie was a breath of fresh air from the outside, a world that was full of adventure, where suppression was just an echo from the past. Richie could see the constant fear in her family's faces at the sound of any vehicle and the expectation that another war would take place in which they would become victims once again.

Richie was keen to explore the area and asked Mirela to show him around.

"Mirela, this landscape has an unfriendly feel to it. I don't know why. There are plenty of trees and the fields look quite fertile, but there is something else lurking. Why did your family settle here?"

"We had no choice. Look around you. What can you see?" Mirela replied.

"A small dwelling over there. Those hills. So what is behind them?"

"More hills!" Mirela laughed. "Have you fuel in your car? If you do, I can show you what we haven't got. One warning—do not wave or greet anybody that I do not wave to first. They are out there waiting to hurt us and will see any sign as a threat."

Mirela showed him places that sent shivers down to his toes and told him stories from the war that only those that had suffered knew about. She told him about Amanita, of how she was forever on the run throughout the war, dodging from one barn to another, killing Serb murderers everywhere as she went.

"And the scar on her cheek?" Richie asked.

Mirela replied, "I was too young to remember how it happen. I was only four or five years, but I was told the story over and over by my grandfather, Amanita's uncle. That's when she got the name—the destroying angel—Amanita Virosa. She never talked about it, but when it happened, they all knew there was big trouble coming, and we fled from Monte Mario to Potocari district.

"There was a Serb patrol out looking for Roma people to kill. They arrive in our village pulling people from their homes into the street and killing them—old people, young people, children. They just murder them without mercy. Grandfather said there was Roma blood everywhere. It was horrible. Sanela disappear and then grandfather hear shots. She had the gun she had put in the wall and she went to the back of the first house in the village and shoot two of the Serb killers. Grandfather said the other men didn't look until they saw one soldier fall down dead next to them. Then they knew. There were seven. She killed three of them, and he could still see another three in the street.

"The soldiers look around to see what happen. She just keep shooting. Then she walk into the street where everyone could see her. It was then the last soldier appear behind her. He grab her by the hair with the knife in his other hand, the same he use to cut the throat of our people. Sanela was only fifteen, you know, but she fight hard to get away just when he was going to cut her neck. The people throw stones at the soldier and he let go. But then it happened. She point her gun at him but it was empty or maybe bullet was stuck. Nobody knows. She drop the gun and she run to one of the dead soldiers.

"She told my grandfather that she could see a knife next to the body but also she could feel the killer soldier so close behind her. She took the knife and was like this." Mirela crouched to demonstrate Amanita's position. "Then she scream and jump up like a wild animal to the soldier. He tried to push her hand with the knife away and he tried to cut her neck with his knife but Sanela was fighting and he cut her face instead. It was too late for him. Sanela was too fast. She push her knife into his belly and pull up hard.

"Grandfather said that everybody stand around her to see the man. I was told he was throwing up blood from his mouth and there were pieces of his inside, but I don't know if that was true. Then she push the people to the side and pick up another soldier's Kalashnikov and shoot all the bullets into the dying soldier's head. Grandfather said she just stood with the gun over his head and shoot and keep shooting until there was nothing left of his head.

"Everybody move away and she stay very quiet, not say a word. Everyone leave her to look down at what she had done. Grandfather said he pull her into the house to treat her cheek. He said she was bleeding too much and she should go to hospital, but she was a Roma and would not be welcome there.

"The Romani that stay here put family and friends in the earth. The dead Serbs were put back in their trucks and drive away to Bosnia border. A village neighbour who can drive took a gun and shoot through the window and doors of the truck with the dead Serbs to look like they were attack, then he drive the truck into a ... how you say ... deep part along the road and put fire to the truck.

"Amanita never speak of what had happened ever again. I think she was ashamed of what she did. She said to everybody the scar was a cat did it. That was the real Amanita."

Richie was silent. He had no idea of Amanita's life before she arrived in Britain. He thought it was a simple case of her eliminating members of the forces that picked on her family. Mirela could see that he was quite shaken and moved away from the subject.

"Richie, grandfather want you to meet some Roma friends. He said he will say you are Sanela's boy and you bring back some Roma blood. That is very important to him, shows much respect. It is all he has from his sister. He also say Richie is not a good Roma name for boy. He say your new name is Guaril. Okay? Now, will you teach me to use a gun? I hope the spirit of Amanita will be in me if I ever need to be hero, like her."

***

As the years passed, Richie and Mirela became very close, and their eventual marriage was agreed upon by all those who should have a say in the matter. Richie's parents arrived in Skelani and were received in grand style as the parents of the man who was Amanita's son, an anomaly in itself. Richie advised them to stay in a hotel for the duration and was pleased to have the time to acquaint them with all that had passed since he had last seen them.

It was at this time that Richie was faced with something else to contend with. Lyn and Alan sat him down and proceeded to tell him a secret they had kept from him for all these years.

"Richie, we have never told you about this because when you started school, we feared that the other kids would bully you if they found out. You see, son, you are actually not British. Well, you are now, but ... " Richie's parents looked at each other and held hands.

"You're both scaring me now. Just come out with whatever you have to say."

Lyn began to well up, and seeing her apprehension, Alan spoke for both of them.

"Richie, you are adopted. Your biological mother was foreign-born."

"What?" He was speechless. What does one say to a revelation like that? So many questions ... where to even begin? "I was born in Britain, wasn't I?" Richie queried, somewhat puzzled and dumbfounded.

Lyn managed to regain her composure. "Yes, of course you were, but your mother wasn't. She was a refugee from Europe and she was dark, like you, and if people knew what she was then you would have had a really hard time. So we pretended that we were your real parents. You see, Richie, I had to have an operation when I was quite small which made me unable to have children. So your father and I decided to adopt, and you were so sweet sitting up in your cot that we couldn't resist you. Your real mother had nowhere to live and the government was very unhelpful. Your mother had no papers to verify her nationality because she was a gypsy from Yugoslavia. Your real father was dead, and she had no support at all even though she was a refugee. She was placed in a camp and died a few months later from pleurisy after a bout of pneumonia. We heard that there were several more in her position.

"Over the years, we never told a soul that you were adopted in case people started to target us and you with all that right wing and anti-immigrant stuff, what with the firebombs and things that people got through their letter boxes. We didn't want to take the chance." Lyn was shaking from worry and looked to Richie for some sign of acceptance and forgiveness.

"Well Mum, Dad, you've done a fantastic job raising me. You've shown me a great deal of love and for that, I'm eternally grateful. I love both of you and have no regrets having you two as my parents, so thank you. I owe you so much!"

Richie leaned forward and put his arms around Lyn and Alan as they burst into tears.

"Mum, you have chosen the right moment to tell me this … the eve of my wedding. Knowing now that I am with my own family and ethnic culture, whatever one wishes to call it, I am now at home. I will be able to wear my new name as if it really does belong to me. So thank you both so much for telling me. I am so happy." Mirela and the newly named Guaril married two days later and the celebrations lasted for another two.

***

Later in the following year, Mirela suggested that they both follow their family tradition—to travel into Italy and help with the harvesting of fruit and olives. Richie was eager, finding that the grinding poverty of scratching a living in Bosnia was rather boring, and Italy sounded like it might be somewhat easier there to make a living.

They set off at the beginning of the season, calling in at any farm they passed. Some had a day's work for them, others a week. But it was also a wonderful opportunity to meet with other groups of Roma people to share and learn.

Richie found himself full of energy, but Mirela was growing more and more tired. She was pregnant, seven months or so. Nonetheless, she continued to toil but at a slower pace until bending to pick the grapes that September became too much. They had made quite a lot of money and had been careful with it in order to buy all the things that a new arrival would need.

October was approaching, and Richie suggested that they return home to the village before the baby arrived. As luck would have it, their car finally gave up with a blown gasket as they travelled up into northern Italy. What was worse, no one was prepared to give them any assistance, "Ha! Help Roma scum? Not a chance!" was a frequent indignity levelled at them as they walked from village to village and town to town.

The road was long and Mirela was really struggling. Now overdue, she settled down by the roadside and prayed that somebody with a kind heart would offer them some help. She gave birth to twins that night under the stars and a full moon. Richie was in awe when she delivered them herself as if it was the normal thing for her to do.

The next morning, having emptied their possessions from their little handcart by the roadside, Richie made off to the nearest small town to buy some food, water and some blankets while Mirela waited in a thicket close by the road for his return.

Richie was found dead in a gully at the side of the road some days later, his wooden handcart loaded with provisions—milk and water, nappies, blankets and a warm woollen stole, all smashed to pieces by a truck driver who did not care to stop. He was a mere two hundred metres from the spot where Mirela waited.

Mirela had started to lose blood, not fast but a slow drain, taking with it much of her strength. Five days she waited for Richie, and on the fifth, she slipped into a deep sleep. Dreams passed through her mind but at last settled when she saw a tall, dark woman approach, dressed in a long, purple, brocaded velvet coat, a large black dog by her side. In the dream, she heard the woman whisper, "Mirela, it is time for you to leave. I will take your babes now. They will be safe with me."

Mirela had no milk left for them, no food for herself, and the first cold, easterly winter wind cooled what remained of her blood faster than she could endure. Mirela died with a tear frozen upon her cheek and her babies still in her arms.

Neither Richie nor Mirela were found for several days. The police had stopped to clear the debris from the wrecked cart, and it was only then that they discovered the corpse of the young man in a gully just off the road, lying exactly where the impact with the truck had left him. It was only on seeing the smashed cart with its contents strewn by the roadside that the police noted some of the items were destined for a mother and baby. After the discovery of Richie, they searched the neighbouring hedgerows and finally found the body of Mirela, but only hers with no sign of her twins. An attempt to find the bodies of the babies by both the police and local people continued for another two weeks but was finally abandoned with the conclusion that they must have been taken and eaten by feral dogs.

Post-mortem evidence showed that Mirela had died only days after having given birth. As the news spread, a feeling of guilt spread through many of the local people who had been so reluctant to aid the couple in their desperate need.

The driver of the truck came forward with remorse. "I thought he was just a tramp or a gypsy, not worth stopping for. I didn't know he was a real person with babies!" His defence failed. Mirela and Richie were buried together, their funeral paid for by the local mayor and gifted a stone to cover their grave.

Morta e Morto
Due Giovani Nel Mondo
Ho Bisogno Di Nostra Aiuto
Per Sempre Sarà Alla Nostra Disgrazia
Dead
Two Young People of the World
In Need Of Our Help
Forever It Will Be Our Disgrace

Epilogue

Amanita's experiences during the Balkan war mirror what the Roma people of Bosnia suffered at the hands of Serbs and Croats who seemed determined to exterminate them in that part of the world. Even now, twenty-five years on, the lives of those people dangle on a string. Children often go without footwear and exist on what scraps they can recycle from waste tips and bins. Many villages have only one tap for drinking water and have no sanitation whatsoever. Education is hit or miss, with many youngsters deprived of schooling. Things are slowly changing for the better with UNICEF and other humanitarian agencies becoming involved, but it will be an uphill struggle for years to come.

About the Author

Barry Harden is the author of a memoir, four fiction novels, two books of poetry and two collections of short stories in the genres of political thriller, fantasy, and satire. An animal rights and environmental protection proponent, he often injects his affinity for such in his writings. Originally from North London, he currently lives in the south of France where he runs a sanctuary for wayward cats when he is not writing.

From the Author

Thank you for purchasing *Amanita Virosa*. I genuinely hope that your reading experience of this book was as enriching as my experience writing it. If you have a moment to spare, I would greatly appreciate it if you could share your thoughts about the book on your preferred online platform for reviews. Additionally, if you're interested in staying updated on my upcoming works, recent blog posts, or joining a community of fellow readers, please visit my website where you can find news about forthcoming projects and sign up for my newsletter. Your support and feedback mean a lot to me. https://www.barryhardenauthor.com.

Sincerely,
Barry Harden

ROUNDFIRE
BOOKS

FICTION

Put simply, we publish great stories. Whether it's literary or popular, a gentle tale or a pulsating thriller, the connecting theme in all Roundfire fiction titles is that once you pick them up you won't want to put them down.
If you have enjoyed this book, why not tell other readers by posting a review on your preferred book site.

Recent bestsellers from Roundfire are:

The Bookseller's Sonnets
Andi Rosenthal
The Bookseller's Sonnets intertwines three love stories
with a tale of religious identity and mystery spanning
five hundred years and three countries.
Paperback: 978-1-84694-342-3 ebook: 978-184694-626-4

Birds of the Nile
An Egyptian Adventure
N.E. David
Ex-diplomat Michael Blake wanted a quiet birding trip
up the Nile – he wasn't expecting a revolution.
Paperback: 978-1-78279-158-4 ebook: 978-1-78279-157-7

Blood Profit$
The Lithium Conspiracy
J. Victor Tomaszek, James N. Patrick, Sr.
The blood of the many for the profits of the few... *Blood Profit$*
will take you into the cigar-smoke-filled room where American
policy and laws are really made.
Paperback: 978-1-78279-483-7 ebook: 978-1-78279-277-2

The Burden
A Family Saga
N.E. David
Frank will do anything to keep his mother and father
apart. But he's carrying baggage – and it might
just weigh him down ...
Paperback: 978-1-78279-936-8 ebook: 978-1-78279-937-5

The Cause
Roderick Vincent
The second American Revolution will be a
fire lit from an internal spark.
Paperback: 978-1-78279-763-0 ebook: 978-1-78279-762-3

Don't Drink and Fly
The Story of Bernice O'Hanlon: Part One
Cathie Devitt
Bernice is a witch living in Glasgow. She loses her way
in her life and wanders off the beaten track looking for the
garden of enlightenment.
Paperback: 978-1-78279-016-7 ebook: 978-1-78279-015-0

Gag
Melissa Unger
One rainy afternoon in a Brooklyn diner, Peter Howland
punctures an egg with his fork. Repulsed, Peter pushes
the plate away and never eats again.
Paperback: 978-1-78279-564-3 ebook: 978-1-78279-563-6

The Master Yeshua
The Undiscovered Gospel of Joseph
Joyce Luck
Jesus is not who you think he is. The year is 75 CE. Joseph
ben Jude is frail and ailing, but he has a prophecy to fulfil …
Paperback: 978-1-78279-974-0 ebook: 978-1-78279-975-7

On the Far Side, There's a Boy

Paula Coston

Martine Haslett, a thirty-something 1980s woman, plays hard on the fringes of the London drag club scene until one night which prompts her to sign up to a charity. She writes to a young Sri Lankan boy, with consequences far and long.
Paperback: 978-1-78279-574-2 ebook: 978-1-78279-573-5

Tuareg

Alberto Vazquez-Figueroa

With over 5 million copies sold worldwide, *Tuareg* is a classic adventure story from best-selling author Alberto Vazquez-Figueroa, about honour, revenge and a clash of cultures.
Paperback: 978-1-84694-192-4

Readers of ebooks can buy or view any of these bestsellers by clicking on the live link in the title. Most titles are published in paperback and as an ebook. Paperbacks are available in traditional bookshops. Both print and ebook formats are available online.

Find more titles and sign up to our readers' newsletter at www.collectiveinkbooks.com/fiction